A · B

MURDER NOW PAY LATER

MURDER NOW PAY LATER

Lauran Paine

Chivers Press • G.K. Hall & Co.
Bath, England   Thorndike, Maine USA

5 8 2 5 9 9

This Large Print edition is published by Chivers Press, England, and by G.K. Hall & Co., USA.

Published in 1998 in the U.K. by arrangement with Robert Hale Ltd.

Published in 1998 in the U.S. by arrangement with Golden West Literary Agency & Robert Hale Ltd.

U.K. Hardcover ISBN 0–7540–3128–4 (Chivers Large Print)
U.S. Softcover   ISBN 0–7838–8300–5 (Nightingale Collection Edition)

The text of this Large Print edition is unabridged.
Other aspects of the book may vary from the original edition.

Set in 16 pt. New Times Roman.

Printed in Great Britain on acid-free paper.

British Library Cataloguing in Publication Data available

Library of Congress Cataloging-in-Publication Data

Paine, Lauran.
    Murder now, pay later / Lauran Paine.
       p. cm.
    ISBN 0–7838–8300–5 (large print : sc : alk. paper)
    1. Large type books.   I. Title.
[PS3566.A34M87   1998]
813′.54—dc21   97–30900

CONTENTS

1	A Brahmin Passes	1
2	Wings West	9
3	A Quiet Interlude	18
4	Dagger Points	28
5	A Sick Man and a Heel	37
6	A List of Suspects	47
7	A Fresh Mystery	56
8	A Dying Man	66
9	Letters of a Ghost	75
10	A Shocker!	85
11	A Climax to Trouble	94
12	No End to Surprises	104
13	Identity of a Murderer!	113
14	A Near Thing	123
15	Return of the Prodigal	133
16	Jared's Scheme	142
17	An Unexpected Windfall	152
18	The Nearing Climax	162
19	Welcome Home!	171
20	A Promise of Amnesty	181
21	The Breath of Death	190
22	The Final Apprehension	200

CHAPTER ONE

A BRAHMIN PASSES

Elizabeth Leeds was a regal lady, tall and statuesque with that variety of copper-gold hair in great abundance one heard of now and again but rarely encountered except possibly in a painting.

Her luminous and large doe-brown eyes had been extolled by newspaper columnists in New York City, while the quality of her carriage, her deportment and evident breeding, had also been favourably commented upon in London and Paris.

That she was wealthy only gilded the lily. There had been any number of discreet admirers after the unfortunate passing of David Leeds six years earlier, all with wealth and position.

Someone once wrote that Elizabeth Leeds had no peer in beauty, no equal in generosity, and no greater self-esteem in the House of Lords.

She hadn't remarried, and that of course kept her in the tattler-columns—not to mention zodiac columns—for five of the six years since the moving-on of her husband. She lived regally in Hyde Park, New York, ancestral seat of the Roosevelts, and maintained a hillside home near Santa Barbara, in California, as well as two cottages, one in Hawaii, the other in Switzerland overlooking one of those delightful little picture-post-card towns.

Once, when nagging reporters badgered crusty and elderly Reginald Morgan— frequently pilloried in newspapers as the second 'Morgan the Pirate'—he had flung round on them with a lion-like roar and had said, whatever Mrs. Leeds chose to do was her business and none of theirs, and furthermore, since her fortune accrued not just through legitimate channels but respectable ones as well, how she disposed of that was also no one's bloody damned business.

Like school-yard bullies the reporters abandoned aloof Elizabeth Leeds for a while to concentrate on old Reginald Morgan, who had been good copy and colourful reading for a number of decades before most people had been on earth.

This did not happen only to Reginald Morgan. Others who lived in Elizabeth's aura also basked, like it or not, in reflected glory, although as Jared Dexter, the attorney, and a handful of Elizabeth's other close friends knew, there was one person who had over the years not appeared upon that glittering social horizon.

Elizabeth had spent a small fortune making sure he would not so appear. Not that she had

2

no feelings for him, she *did* have, but her second secret, known to perhaps only one or two, including her dead husband and Jared Dexter, would have destroyed a myth of youthfulness, and that was one thing Elizabeth could not compel herself even to think about. Her vanity was enormous. Right or wrong, like other ravishing beauties here and gone, Elizabeth spent large sums keeping youthful. Like Marlene Dietrich and a few others who could afford it, she outwitted the ageing process handily.

Then she was murdered.

It stunned the Western world. There were always plenty of envious people, mostly female or Leftist, who deplored her extravagances, her beauty, the ivory-tower atmosphere she lived and moved in. Even when she had endowed an orphans' home in Vietnam she was attacked. The Leftists said she did that to salve a capitalistic conscience, and the equally vociferous and fuzzy-thinking multitude of envious people said she had done it in the grand manner of some decadent duchess casting crusts to the pitiful creatures her country had made orphans of in its savage Vietnamese war.

But mostly, people were stunned and astonished at her murder, because in general people were interested in her as a personality, almost an institution, that represented something richer and more grand than the jet-

3

set. Elizabeth Leeds managed very often to be compared to a genuinely regal Elizabeth, which only added to the fairy-tale glamour that surrounded her.

Dead, she managed for seven days to crowd an impending great holocaust between two super-powers off the front pages, leaving the nuclear sabre-rattlers to hurl their grisly prognostications, threats and promises, almost in a world-wide vacuum.

As Jared told old Reginald Morgan, it was very doubtful if a woman who had never written a book, made a motion picture, produced a love-child of unknown paternity, or who had actually done anything really remarkable except to be endowed by Nature with a fabulous beauty, and to have inherited from her international-industrialist husband an enormous fortune, had ever before so captured the imagination, for better or for worse, of the world.

Reginald's reply had been, banker-like, more directly to the point. 'Be that as it may, I suppose you now intend to bring forth George Alexander. I tell you, Jared, unless I am very wrong George Alexander is going to hate you to his dying day if you do bring him to New York.'

Jared's predictable, and in fact his only, answer to that prediction was blunt. 'There is simply nothing else to be done, and whether *I* bring him here or not, he will inevitably have to

4

arrive. You know that as well as I do.'

'*She* wouldn't have wanted it.'

'Reginald, *she* can't stop it. Not any longer. And I'm surprised you'd make such an emotional statement.'

Old Morgan coldly smiled. 'Didn't you know, Jared, that I was in love with her for thirty years?'

Jared Dexter, acting in his capacity as the attorney for the late and presumably lamented Mrs. Elizabeth Leeds, queen, dowager, and eternal—almost—arbiter of *real* high society, was under legal edict to file the Will for probate, to meet the press at the Leeds' Hyde Park home, and to make full arrangements for a funeral that couldn't have been kept simple even if Elizabeth had desired it, which she probably hadn't, actually, although there were no specific directions left behind among her personal letters, papers and directives to this effect.

But he still, for almost two weeks, was able to avoid mentioning George Alexander, and when queried by old Morgan *sotto voce* as they stood in the huge and glittering cathedral during the Last Rites eulogy, heads bowed, he had simply said, 'No time yet. I'm not avoiding it at all, there just hasn't been a moment for anything but these arrangements.'

'I'll be watching with interest,' whispered Morgan, and lapsed into a proper head-hung reverence when a nearby spectator had turned

5

and glared.

But even after Elizabeth had been entombed—not *in* the ground, *above* it—Dexter's days were still filled with the details of a lavish life spanning a surprising number of years. Elizabeth had, woman-like, rarely finished anything although she was a prodigious starter. An example was the tangled mess of the orphanage's financial status. Elizabeth had sent cheques whenever she'd happened to remember orphanages were a dead financial weight. She had paid other obligations in a like manner. Jared finally brought in an old friend, a quite successful and respected accountant named Frederick Steele, to make a full-time in-depth study of Elizabeth's badly bungled financial affairs.

Then, too, there were the more personal details of those four homes, their salaried retainers who clamoured for clarification of their status, understandably, and the myriad annoying, small but pertinent matters arising therefrom.

Finally, with their notorious punctuality, representatives of the United States Internal Revenue Service arrived, clasping attaché cases to their worsted bosoms, and bringing along any number of Inheritance Tax tables, forms and time-limits.

Jared tried twice to get away. The first time three days after the murder, the second time the third week afterwards. He never quite

6

managed it, and meanwhile Reginald called from his walnut-panelled office on the twentieth floor of the Carleton Manhattan International Bank to make insistent suggestions and pointed reminders.

'Jared,' he said the last time, almost four weeks after the funeral, 'if you can't do it yourself, then you must send someone else. The bank has all these damned accruing accounts and something has simply got to be done. I don't care how busy the other details have kept you. You aren't enhancing your image with me, you know, by demonstrating this complete inability to get on top of things.'

Dexter's reply had been a study in quiet calm. 'Reginald, George Alexander is not going to fly to the moon, and as executor I simply can't relegate important details to just anyone, and go to the West Coast. As for the financial details, I'll ask Fred Steele to confer with the bank—meaning you. Otherwise, what possible harm can arise from letting the money pile up?'

'That,' snapped back crusty old Morgan, 'is the comment of an idiot! In the first place, we're setting up a separate tax-accounting, and in the second place *someone* has to make the major decision. She didn't leave her fortune to me or to you, so as her adviser I'm hogtied. As for you, being executor of the estate, the bank lawyers tell me, limits your power too. So— you've got to go out there and get George

Alexander and bring him here. And within the next few days. Otherwise the bank will simply have to go before the court and either request it be appointed executor in your place—which it should have been anyway—or else it must petition the court to light a damned fire under you.'

When Morgan had finished he slammed down the telephone.

Jared drove to the Hyde Park mansion, located the accountant Steele out by the pool, tie-less and coat-less, working at a table heaped with papers beneath a gay-striped beach-umbrella, and dropped into a nearby chair as he said, 'Morgan is getting disagreeable. I'll have to fly to the West Coast within the next day or two. Anything you'll need me for, the next couple of days?'

Steele, a football-player type who had grey eyes, a long, thin mouth, and a nose that had been broken and re-set several times, below a shock of close-cropped curly light hair, looked over with a slow grin and said, 'Yeah, one thing: tell someone high up to keep those damned policemen from going through every drawer in the place and further disturbing a file-system that was inaugurated in a windstorm.' Steele shook his head. 'Not really, Jared. *Bon voyage.* By the way—do you know what you'll say when you get out there?'

'I know. I'll say go and shave and bathe and put some decent clothes on and let's go back to

8

New York.'

'Will it be enough?'

'How the hell do I know, Fred? I'm worth three-quarters of a million dollars and I'm forty. *He* is worth—who really and truly knows?—perhaps eighty million, and he is thirty years old. Ten years and different philosophies used not to make that much difference, but they do now. Generation gaps keep getting shorter and shorter.'

'Well, like I said, Jared: *Bon voyage.*'

CHAPTER TWO

WINGS WEST

George Alexander was large and wide-shouldered without actually projecting that impression. He was a strikingly handsome man with deep-set, grave blue eyes that somehow put people who knew who his mother was, in mind of her.

His hair, however, was black, like his brows and lashes, and since Jared had never known his father—old Reginald Morgan had, and he had also steadfastly refused to discuss him even with Jared—he could only assume that the hint of darkness had come from that parent.

Jared *did* know, although Elizabeth had also never mentioned it in his presence, that George

9

Alexander's father had married Elizabeth when he had been eighteen to her sixteen, and that marriage had lasted until her twenty-fifth year, when George had been born. Then the man known as Alexander had disappeared and had never been seen again, assumed to have abandoned his wife and infant son.

That had been Elizabeth Leeds' foremost secret. That she'd been married right out of school and that she had had a son out in California who was now thirty years old, quiet, thoughtful, but in ways she'd never tried to fathom, also hard and unyielding.

He showed those last two attributes now, sitting glass in hand upon the picturesque balcony of his hillside house overlooking the town of Santa Barbara, and the great blue expanse of Pacific Ocean beyond.

He said, 'I was there, Mr. Dexter. It was an impressive funeral.' He drained the glass, set it upon a little rattan table and swung his handsome face with its brooding look. 'What do you want of me?'

It was such an asinine question, and the man's manner and mood were so languidly calm, Jared Dexter had to wrestle down his rising irritation when he replied. 'George, there is absolutely nothing simple about your inheritance. Morgan at the bank needs decisions and you are the only person who can step in now.'

'I was her only heir?'

'Yes. When we reach my office I'll show you all the papers.'

'What about my father?'

Jared blinked. 'Well, what about him? As far as I know he's been out of the picture since a month or two before you were born.'

'Did my mother tell you that?'

'Well no, but I've been her attorney for fifteen years, George, and never once in all that time has she heard from him, and there was absolutely nothing in her desk or files about him. If you wish, I can file to force him to show cause why he would try to break her will.'

'Care for another gin-and-tonic, Mr. Dexter?'

'No thanks.'

The tall man unwound up out of his chair with a loose, easy grace. He wore a short-sleeved knitted shirt that showed powerful arms and wrists. There was a gay handkerchief knotted around his bronzed throat. He was handsome, extremely so, more so in fact than most movie idols, but there was a strange aloofness to him, almost as though he were at this moment going through an act he'd rehearsed so many times it bored him.

'Mind if I get another?' he said, gliding in his white tennis shoes towards an open french window that made up the entire wall behind the breeze-swept gallery.

Jared shook his head. 'Not at all.' He watched Alexander pass back into the house

11

towards the rattan bar and go to work, and he had a feeling of frustration that for some reason made him think of Fred Steele's crooked smile when they'd last been together. Fred had seemed somehow to know what Jared was going to be up against on the West Coast but of course that was ridiculous because Fred didn't know George Alexander, had never in fact even seen the man.

Through the glass door Alexander said softly, 'Mr. Dexter, I have a trust fund as you very well know, that pays me three thousand dollars monthly. I have my home, my boat down at the yacht club, and if, as the newspapers claim, the estate is in excess of a hundred million dollars—'

'Closer to eighty, I think,' put in Jared, twisting to watch the younger, larger man.

'All right, eighty. It's too much and it's too like a collar of solid lead.'

Dexter's exasperation slipped a rung. 'Listen to me, George; your mother hired me when I was younger than you are right now, and whatever her reasons—although I think we both know them—I've been your—well—your guardian ever since. I've done my utmost to give you good advice. I've looked after your interests like an elder brother, and now I'm telling you that you simply have *got* to return with me to New York.'

Alexander turned with two glasses in his hands, strolled out and handed one to Jared.

He faintly smiled. 'You're going to have high blood pressure.' Then he resumed his slouched position in the chair where an aged and bloody-flowering hibiscus grew up the side of the Spanish-style house and had a strong foothold over the edge of the gallery.

'What in the hell will I do with eighty million dollars?' he asked, and hoisted the glass as though the answer didn't even concern him. 'Have I ever told you what I think of those phoney jet-setters, and those white-tied glittering people who are so internationally exotic?'

'No.'

'Would you like to hear, Mr. Dexter?'

'No.'

George turned and laughed. His teeth were perfect, his laugh a slow rumble. When he smiled the brooding look disappeared and he looked closer to twenty than thirty. 'You're a good man, Mr. Dexter, but well on the way to becoming a stuffed-shirt—like old Morgan.'

'You don't even know old Morgan,' said Jared, annoyed.

'Sure I do. I saw him at the funeral whispering to you. I've seen him in Washington at the United Nations galas. I've seen him in newspapers and I've read his sententious pronouncements on everything from economics to world order. I know him as well as though he had come out once a year as you used to do when I was in school, to pat my

13

head and make sure my funds were in order. And he isn't a relevant human being.'

Jared picked up the drink he didn't want and tasted it. George Alexander made a really remarkable martini. 'You've got to come back with me,' he said, and turned to look at the breathtaking view. 'You're too comfortable here, George; you can't just be a parasite, you know.'

'Why not? That's what I've been educated to be.'

'No, not quite. You had your law degree.'

'But I never took the bar examinations and I've never practised.'

Jared forced himself to relax. This wasn't going to be easy and he'd never had any illusions about that. But if he had to sit there in the lovely sun and shadow drinking George into a stupor, he was going to get the man back to New York with him.

'Mr. Dexter, tell me—'

'Damn it, George, I'm not all that much older. Just call me Jared, will you?'

'Sorry, I had no idea men of forty were so touchy. I'd always thought men wanted to be forty. Sorry again. Now tell me about the murder.'

Jared's light grip on the glass-stem tightened. 'There isn't much to tell. She was...'

'Go ahead. I sorrowed. Who wouldn't? After all, she *was* my mother. But not seeing her very much in my life made it different. I

14

read that much in the papers; she was strangled with her own hair. Bizarre, eh? Samson apparently wasn't the only one whose vanity for his hair got him into trouble. What have the police got to say?'

'I can't really say, George. I've been so damned busy with other things. Being an executor in this case is a genuine nightmare. She wasn't much of an organizer and she was an even worse book-keeper. All I know is probably no more than you've read. It was a man, and he had considerable strength. He got into the house somehow—although that wouldn't have been any great accomplishment, the place has more doors and windows than a castle—and got to her dressing-room. There, he caught her from behind as she sat before the dressing-table preparing for bed, her hair down, wrapped the strands round her neck and killed her.'

George continued to sit like stone, staring out over the distant, blue ocean, highball glass in hand, his unwound body loose and gangling. 'There are more details,' he eventually said quietly. 'The police know more than just the obvious facts.'

'Perhaps, George, but as I've told you, I've been much too otherwise involved to ask around.'

Alexander suddenly rose, stepped back through the opening in the glass wall, picked a paper off an end-table, came back and dropped it into Dexter's lap. Without speaking he then resumed his seat and finished his drink.

The paper was a letter addressed to George Alexander by an official of the New York State penal commission, giving the dry statistics about a prisoner identified by a long number, whose name was Harold Alexander. Jared leaned over to read and re-read this letter. Then he raised his eyes to the date the letter had been dictated and finally said, 'How did you find him, George?'

'Does that matter? He was released from prison three days before the murder.' George's blue eyes sought Dexter. 'What kind of parents did I really deserve, Jared? Not what kind did I *get*, but what kind did I *deserve*.'

Dexter bent to examine the letter again, and after he'd put it gently aside and picked up his martini he said, 'That's something I can't answer, George. Anyway, this doesn't mean there had to be a connection.'

'Beautiful coincidence though, wouldn't you say?'

'That's for the police to thresh out.' Dexter upended his glass, put it on top of the letter and leaned back to gaze out at the ocean again, and all those red-tiled roofs in their lovely tree-girt settings below where the town sprawled in its beautiful dished-out small cove.

'When does the New York flight leave?' asked George.

Jared's tight lips loosened a little. 'We can

16

take the one leaving at five this afternoon, or we can take the one leaving at six tomorrow morning. I'd suggest the latter flight. It'll put us back in Manhattan with plenty of time to shower and change and get back on our feet.' He sat waiting for a reply but none came for a very long while, and in that interim a white foreign sports car came whipping along the mountainside-road heading either for the Alexander dwelling or one of the few other rare eagle's eyries that clung this far up on the slopes behind and above Santa Barbara. They both watched. Jared was annoyed by the thought that some friend of George's might be arriving to intrude. But the little car only bleated twice and whipped straight on past, heading back along the curve of slope where another few houses stood, partially hidden in trees and flourishing tall bushes.

'In the morning, then,' said George finally, and unwound the third time up out of his chair with that graceful but hardly dignified way he had of both sitting and rising. 'Come along; we'll go down to the yacht club for dinner.'

Dexter rose but didn't follow his host. Instead, he halted the other man in the doorway by saying, 'George, just answer one question: Had you already made up your mind to go back with me?'

Alexander flashed that handsome, slow smile. 'Yeah. When you called from the airport that you were coming over, Jared, I went and packed a couple of bags. I'm psychic, didn't you know?'

Dexter thought of something a lot less flattering and perhaps a lot more descriptively correct, but he didn't say it.

'Don't be mad,' laughed Alexander. 'I tease people, Jared, but I don't hurt them. I learned twenty years ago not to hurt people. Okay?'

Jared didn't answer. He didn't want to and he didn't have to. Over the years as he'd watched George Alexander mature from rich, lonely and deprived childhood to manhood, he'd always felt uncomfortable about the hurt he'd seen in those eyes that were so like his mother's eyes. George had spoken the truth just now; he had learned a long time ago what hurt was.

He said, 'Those damned martinis were strong,' and followed his host inside the house. 'Where do I shower and change?'

CHAPTER THREE

A QUIET INTERLUDE

The flight back was uneventful, cramped and swift. Even so, George had made one enlightening comment that Jared remembered with whimsical interest, so he couldn't have said the trip was boring, as most flights are.

18

They had been discussing the friends of George's mother, none of whom George knew, actually, although now and then he mentioned a name or nodded with recognition when Jared mentioned one. Elizabeth had always been surrounded by those extremely well-off and glittering people. Some, the ones her son knew by name only from repetitive mention in newspapers, were Elizabeth's closest friends.

It had been when Jared, mentioning the return from Europe of Elizabeth the previous year, had said how her loyal entourage had returned with her, more like a queen and her retinue than a wealthy American widow, that George had said, 'Some people have to have adulation as others need food, and they can absorb inordinate amounts of it without ever having to put out any themselves. It's like nourishment to them and no matter how much they get, they can't expend one bit. It's pitiful, Jared.'

This, like most of the other things George said on that flight, had its foundation, Jared knew, in the bizarre mother-son relationship, and although George never openly displayed actual hostility towards his dead mother, Jared had to wonder if, down deep, it wasn't there in ample amounts.

When they taxied from the airport it was raining, the sky was overcast, the city was a wet explosion of light that flattened against the underbelly of the lowering heavens, and

George said he liked the smell of wet pavement.

It was necessary for Jared to go all the way to Hyde Park with George not only because Elizabeth's servants didn't know who he was, but also because they were like the vast majority of other people in their total ignorance that she'd ever had a child.

But after Jared had gone to all that trouble, and the servants had stood dumbfounded looking at him, George had refused to stay at the mansion and had ridden back into the city with George where he engaged rooms at a hotel.

The following morning, Jared, driving his own car, picked George up at the hotel and returned to the Hyde Park place with him. Frederick Steele was already there. In fact he was having coffee on the Grecian terrace overlooking the magnificent swimming pool in an aura of thoughtfulness that Jared noticed at once when they met and he introduced George to Fred.

Steele would have got them coffee but Jared declined on the grounds that he had to hurry back, and George's excuse was simply that he'd eaten breakfast only a short while earlier.

Jared led the way to that shaded large table where Fred worked, waited for the other men to be seated, then said, 'We might as well establish the precedent right here; from time to time we're going to have to have conferences, we three. Fred, how are things shaping up?'

Steele put aside his coffee and smiled apologetically as he said, 'Slow, Jared. Mrs. Leeds evidently had something against an orderly existence.' He looked at George and said a bit hastily, 'Not that it isn't common. In my experience a great many people who have no need to mind their pennies refuse to be burdened by details. I guess it's all right, only when they die it sure makes a mess for others to sweat over.'

'But you've made progress,' prompted Jared.

Steele, gazing at the neat piles of papers on his table, nodded. 'Slow progress, Jared, but progress.'

George, sitting slouched, said, 'Find anything odd, Mr. Steele?' and when Fred's eyes lifted enquiringly, George made a light gesture towards all those mounds of paper. 'Anything that could have been blackmail, possibly, or anything that seemed alien to her pattern of life.'

Steele understood. 'No, I wouldn't say so, Mr. Alexander. The police had a man here for two days—while you were gone, Jared—but compared to him the sphinx is a regular blabbermouth.'

Jared was interested. 'Did he take anything away with him, Fred?'

'No, but I doubt if he'd have done that anyway. Not without getting your permission. However, he *did* make a few notes.'

'About what?'

Steele showed that little dry smile again. 'He didn't say.'

George seemed satisfied. 'Nice to know they're on the job.'

Jared's reaction was different. 'It sounds as though they may be more interested in Elizabeth than in her murderer. I'll look into that.' He rose. 'Anything else, Fred?'

There wasn't, so Steele and George Alexander went out to Jared's car with him. To Jared's suggestion that George ride into the city with him, George said he thought he'd poke about the mansion for a bit.

Jared's desire had been to take George to old Reginald Morgan's office. He mentioned that, but quite gently, since George's reaction each time old Morgan was brought up, had been if not downright hostile, then at least scornful.

George nodded, saying he'd see Morgan presently, and Jared let it go at that. After he'd driven off a servant came to say a newsman was calling. The servant seemed to be in doubt as to whether Fred or George should take the call. The only resident for some time now, since the passing of the man's mistress, had been Fred Steele, and servant-like, the man had fastened his loyalty to Steele.

As it turned out, Steele *did* take the call. As he and George stood out there in the light drizzle Fred said, 'You know, if you'd like to buy a little time to yourself, I can go to tell him

22

there's nothing new to report.'

George studied Steele for a moment in that direct, impassive manner he had, then nodded. 'Good idea. I'll have a look around the grounds.'

Steele returned to the house, servant trailing in his wake, told his lie over the telephone, rang off and turned as the servant said, 'Mr. Steele, is he *really* her son?'

Fred smiled. 'That's what Mr. Dexter told you, isn't it?'

'Yes, sir. But there have been stories, you know, about how lawyers and others ... when there's a lot of money involved ... bring in someone.'

Fred's smile faded except in the depths of his eyes. 'I'd be careful of that kind of talk if I were you. Mr. Dexter wouldn't like it.'

'Oh, I'm not actually saying—'

'Yes, I know. But suppose you made a remark like that to one of those snoopy reporters? See where it could lead; you'd not only be out of a job, but you'd be putting both Mr. Dexter and Mr. Alexander in a rather awkward spot. I think they'd want your hide for it, too. And by the way; I'm only a book-keeper around here. From now on it's Mr. George Alexander.'

'Yes, sir.'

The drizzle continued, the day was grey, but warm and in an indefinable way, pleasant. There was a subdued, silent feel to it, as though

23

something momentous has recently occurred and now was the time of ebb-tide and langour.

It was an excellent time to walk the grounds; there was no sun-glare, but, more important to someone who prized privacy, with Elizabeth no longer there, a flame to draw the moths, the grounds, like the great house, had an atmosphere of peace.

They covered several acres, actually, and were splendidly landscaped. There were trees and shrubs and beds of flowers, recently set out by a gardener who kept to himself, living in quarters off the three-car garage, and whose ghost-like comings and goings seemed as alien to the rest of the Leeds establishment as one could imagine.

However much the man might be a recluse, he was a genius at his trade. Where others might have given up over a rock outcropping, he'd managed to encourage growth by putting soil in the crevices and pockets, and the rock looked as gay and worthwhile now as George could imagine it had once looked drab and sullen.

The grass too, was emerald colour instead of pale green, the result, no doubt, of pulverized dressing. It was weedless, which was no simple accomplishment in springtime New York, and it was soft to the touch.

Then there was a bed of bulbs, green fingers standing erect above the slight swellings at ground-level. It was too early yet to say what they might be, iris or tulips, but judging by everything else, they would blossom into a riot of soul-satisfying colour.

And there was also the stone wall on the property line, visible here and there through an evergreen growth that nearly obscured it, behind the bulb bed. That was where George picked up the shoe-heel. It was also where he traced out the route someone had used reaching the yonder stone wall and scaling it. By lifting evergreen boughs he found the fresh scores where small nails had scratched up the rock.

Later, around in front again, he strolled all along the front of the house studying window-sills and panes. There were no marks, if that was what he sought, and where the glassed-in three walls of the conservatory let daylight inside, where more flowers and shrubs grew in stone beds built along each wall, with one wall facing front, he stood the longest. But the putty was old, the panes were all intact, so if access had been gained here it must have been achieved through an unlocked door.

Finally, he returned to the area of the marble pool and dropped into a chair as Frederick Steele rocked back, grinned and lit a cigarette as he said, 'Beautiful, isn't it?'

George nodded. 'Very.' Then he said, 'Were you here at a party, ever?'

Fred shook his head. 'Wasn't in that circle, George. It takes time to get there. I'm three years older than you are.'

George's blue eyes with their metallic sheen, looked interested. 'Jared told you how old I am?'

'Yes. In a casual conversation.'

'But he came to the parties, I suppose?'

Steele's gaze narrowed very slightly. 'What's on your mind?'

'Murder.'

Steele inhaled, exhaled, studied the tip of a pencil and said, 'Skip Jared Dexter. He lost more than he could have gained. Besides, as I've heard it said, your mother took him fresh out of law school and made him rich. He'd undoubtedly have become even richer had she lived.'

'Any other ideas, Fred?'

'I'm an accountant, not a cop. Sorry.'

The smoky blue eyes lingered, then passed slowly to the papers on the table. 'What is all that? Household accounts?'

'Mostly, yes. But there are some personal things—like that orphanage in Vietnam. Nothing, actually, that will make any difference in the size of your inheritance, George. But it sure would have been better if Mrs. Leeds had kept a private secretary. Her personal affairs were a mess.'

'You're winning though, I take it?'

'I'm winning, yes.' Steele's gaze was quizzical. Obviously, he couldn't come to any conclusion about this powerful, black-headed, unusual person sitting with him. 'I shall probably wind it up by the end of next week.'

'After that?'

Steele kept studying George Alexander. 'Well, I have a private accounting business. Not large, but adequate. Actually, I took this job because Jared asked it.'

'You two are friends?'

'Yes. Have been for a number of years.' Steele's smile flashed again. 'We went to the same university. He was an upper classman. We became good friends then. Jared's tops in my book.'

George rose, plunged his hands into trouser pockets and turned slightly to glance over where the bulb bed was distantly visible. He didn't say a word, and after a moment of standing like that, he turned and strolled on into the house.

Frederick Steele finished his cigarette gazing at the french windows through which Alexander had passed. Whatever his feelings about Alexander, his thoughts were fairly readable in the wry, calculating expression he wore.

Then he stubbed out his cigarette, took up the pencil and went back to work, while the drizzle stopped entirely, the clouds began moving easterly with a heaving, ponderous slowness, and a very faint little warm breeze came to ruffle the papers on Steele's table.

CHAPTER FOUR

DAGGER POINTS

Reginald Morgan didn't smile when Jared ushered George Alexander into the office, although he did rise to shake hands. Actually, old Morgan looked annoyed. Perhaps he had some justification. He'd called Jared the day before to be unpleasant, and Jared had told him George Alexander had arrived in the city a day earlier and old Morgan's roar had quivered with indignation.

'Why haven't you brought him here, Jared, confound it all!'

The answer Jared had given was what kept Morgan from smiling now, as he eased back into his chair and put a fierce and domineering glare upon Alexander. Jared had said, 'Listen; this isn't Russia. I can't send a couple of gorillas over to muscle him into a car for delivery to your office, Reginald. I told him, the day we arrived back here, you wished to see him. He said he'd see you presently. Now that's all I can do.'

Morgan, an immensely powerful and somewhat Tartar-like old man, clenched his hands on top of the magnificent mahogany desk and said nothing until he'd completed his study of George Alexander. Jared, mildly

28

embarrassed by what seemed needless rudeness, became occupied with a speck of lint on his knee.

Then Morgan spoke. 'Mr. Alexander, your inheritance entails a complex list of investments which require constant watching and guiding. Under your mother, this bank—and I—served as trustee and adviser. But of course that is changed now, and hereafter you'll have to give us your decisions in order that we may continue to function in the same capacity—providing, of course, you wish us to so function.'

George crossed his legs at the ankles, pushed out his long legs and said nothing. His gaze was direct, stone-steady, and inscrutable.

Jared, watching this silent duel, fidgeted and waited. He'd had some earlier misgivings about how these two would react to one another, but that really was beyond his realm.

Old Morgan spluttered, reddening under the gunmetal gaze of the younger man. 'Well, confound it, what have you to say, Mr. Alexander?'

'Let's start out by saying, Mr. Morgan, that when people start out by going over me with hobnails, I have a tendency to want to knock them out of their chairs.'

Jared was flabbergasted. He'd expected some snideness on both sides, but no physical violence. He drew straight up in the chair, but if his surprise was sudden, old Morgan's was

29

even more so. He looked as though someone had just doused him with cold water. It could be assumed, too, that no one had spoken to Morgan the Pirate like that in many years. Perhaps they *never* had. Now, he slammed both palms on the desk and shot up out of his chair, pale eyes flaming, red face quivering with indignation.

'Get out of here,' he said in a loud voice. 'Get out right this instant!'

Alexander sat on, still relaxed and comfortable. 'Sit down,' he said quietly, and when Morgan bristled still more he repeated it. '*Sit down!*'

For three seconds Jared held his breath. Morgan was furious. Jared, who had known him all Jared's professional life, had never seen the old man so angry.

George came up out of his chair with that animal looseness, ambled over and leaned towards Morgan across the desk. 'For the last time, Mr. Morgan—*sit down!*'

Morgan sat.

George didn't show anything in his face as he said, still using that soft-quiet tone of voice, 'There's nothing to be so angry about. You tried and I didn't take it. So now we understand each other. That's all. As for the inheritance, yes, I want you and the bank to continue to administer it. You are both supremely capable.' George went back to his chair, sat, crossed his legs exactly as before, and smiled gently at old Morgan. 'If I can't always come here when you need me, I'll see that you'll always know how to reach me. I don't live in New York and if you gave me a Manhattan Island I still wouldn't live here, but that shouldn't make things too difficult for us, should it?'

Morgan's face was less florid now and his eyes held a look of bafflement in their moving depths. He shook his head in reply to Alexander's statement, then sighed and leaned upon the desk again. Whatever his true feelings, he was at least for now, going along with the quiet behaviour Alexander had initiated.

'I have a list of questions we need answers to,' he said, staring at Alexander, his voice still rough from recent wrath. 'Also, if you'll spend a few days here in the bank with us, we'll see that you are brought up to date on the Leeds Estate financial affairs, which are complex, and larger in scope and wealth than almost any other estate we handle. Can you do that, Mr. Alexander?'

George took his time answering. What he finally said, though, indicated that he'd hung fire for a very specific reason. 'I don't know, Mr. Morgan. I've never been very apt at high finance. Never had much feeling for it, nor have I ever felt it was worthwhile.'

Jared flinched. That statement struck at the very heart of old Morgan's lifelong

31

convictions, down-grading them in a manner that left the impression George Alexander was contemptuous of great fortunes, the people who possessed them—and the people who administered them.

Reginald Morgan sat hunched and staring, hands interlocked on the desk again. Finally, when Jared expected fresh anger, old Morgan said, 'To each his own, Mr. Alexander. But I'll still need your decisions from time to time. And Mr. Alexander—however you may feel, and I think I detect some kind of foolishness, radicalism or something close to it, in your attitude—remember that you have over eighty million dollars, less inheritance taxes of course, and so forth, so like it or not you are one of the richest young men in America.'

Morgan leaned back in flinty triumph. He'd had his say, had hurled his barb, had driven home his point, and if it didn't entirely ameliorate his indignation, it nevertheless helped a good deal.

George smiled at him that slow-gathering, warm smile. 'I'll learn to live with that until I decide what's to be done. Otherwise, I've got worlds of confidence in you.'

'Is that so? Flattering though it may be, it would be even more so if you'd explain just how you can have all this confidence since we don't know one another—and I'm sure, having known your mother so well, that she never tutored you along these lines.'

George's reaction to sarcasm was similar to his reaction to being shouted at; he met it head on. Still smiling, he said, 'Mr. Morgan, in my lifetime I've had ample reason, and plenty of time over week-ends in boarding schools when I was the only kid who had no home to go to, for being interested in what kind of people there are in this world. On that basis I'd judge you to be overbearing, very self-satisfied, honest in the good old-fashioned New England way, and tough at driving a bargain. But essentially, I'd say you are honest and dedicated.' George gave his big shoulders a slight hitch. 'If I'm wrong, you will rob me blind. If that happens I'll put you in a wheelchair for the rest of your life. But I'm not very often wrong about people. Now you know why I have confidence in you.' George rose, shoved his hands into trouser-pockets and stopped smiling. 'And you are so right, Mr. Morgan, my mother never tutored me—about you or anything else. Jared, let's go!'

Morgan didn't rise as Jared came up to his feet. He was looking at George Alexander as though he'd just come face to face with something from the Palaeolithic Age. He let George get completely out of the office, into his reception room, before he said, 'Jared ...?'

Dexter was in the open doorway. He looked back a trifle uncomfortably, then murmured something to George, stepped back into the office, eased the door closed and said, 'Don't say it, Reginald. The walls may be thin and moreover, this was your conference, not mine. All I had to do was introduce you to him.'

Morgan spluttered. 'I don't understand.'

Jared didn't attempt any explanation although he could have; after all, Jared had watched George Alexander grow up; he knew him better than his own mother had known him. But the plain truth was that George didn't understand him either.

'Reginald, you were disagreeable when we first walked in here. I know—you had reason. But this time it wasn't some bank employee nor some businessman-supplicant. And one other thing: I don't think he was just making talk.'

'I've never been threatened like that before in my life!'

'Don't worry about it.'

Morgan's brows dropped ominously. His eyes beneath flashed a quick, hot fire. '*Worry* about it? Don't be ridiculous. I've met braggarts and pseudo tough-guys before. I know how to handle them.'

'Reginald, this one isn't any tough-guy, pseudo or otherwise, and he's no braggart either. Please, Reginald, don't keep trying to dominate him. You'll never do it. Now I've got to run. See you later.'

Down in the blustery street where shreds of soiled clouds were being pushed in all directions by a high wind, Jared stopped and looked at George Alexander.

'Well, I don't think all that was necessary, but on the other hand I don't entirely blame you.'

George wasn't interested. 'The variety of people is endless,' he said, watching passers-by, 'but bullies are usually pretty transparent. We'll get along, Morgan and I.' He dropped his gaze. 'Anything else you want me to do while we're here in the city?'

'Not particularly. Can I drive you back?'

'No thanks. I want to do a little nosing about.'

Jared nodded. 'Let me guess—the police.'

'For a starter,' said George. 'And something else. Care to make a try for that too?'

Jared hesitated. He thought he knew but didn't think it would lie well nor sound well, if he mentioned it. 'No, not this time.'

George, watching his face, smiled. 'You're a nice guy, Jared. Money-hungry but nice. You can guess what else I want. That man who was released from prison last month.'

'Good luck,' said Jared, faintly reddening. 'George, don't work so hard at laying people's souls bare. You'll make more friends by keeping the private assessments to yourself. I'm not money-hungry. I once was, but that passed when I began crowding up close to forty. It used to be enough to be a millionaire, but now it no longer is. The trouble is, I still think in terms of one million, and I'm near enough to it be satisfied with life. Not money-hungry any more.'

George smiled. 'Come by the mansion tonight. I'll move out there this afternoon. By the way, have you any objection if I ask Fred Steele to move in and live there while he's working on the accounts?'

'No. But he might have.'

'Is he married or something?'

Jared had to smile. 'He's not married, but as to the "or something" that may be why he likes to prowl about after dark.'

They parted, George strolling northward with that loose-easy gait of his, Jared Dexter towards a taxi-stand. He had no desire to go to the Hyde Park mansion that night, which is why he'd side-stepped any direct reply to the invitation. He'd had quite enough of George Alexander for a while.

But when he reached the office there was a call from Reginald Morgan to be answered, and when the banker came on the line, Jared sighed because he knew he wasn't going to get the respite after all.

'Jared, I just had a telephone call from Steele out at the Leeds place. He thought you would be at my office. He said there was a stranger out there, half drunk and demanding to see young Alexander.'

Jared glanced at his wrist. It was still no more than noon, which meant George wouldn't be returning to the mansion, probably, until much later. He said, 'Thank you, Reginald. I'll get hold of Steele and tell him to get rid of the man.'

'Yes, of course,' exclaimed old Morgan. 'Probably some tramp-friend of Alexander's. I tell you, Jared, it's beyond me where that man gets his nasty disposition. Certainly not from Elizabeth.'

'Thanks again,' said Jared, unwilling to be drawn into this kind of conversation. He rang off, put down the telephone and hung up both hat and coat, flung his attaché case upon a rich, dark leather couch, and turned to stand gazing out of the fifteenth-floor window of his law-suite.

He had a feeling that instead of being able gracefully to get clear of the Leeds matter, he was going to be sucked into it deeper than Elizabeth had ever wished, and that he had ever wanted.

CHAPTER FIVE

A SICK MAN AND A HEEL

Jared still could have avoided going to Hyde Park. He'd reached Fred Steele earlier to say Alexander probably wouldn't be back for hours, and Steele had told him of the man who was still there, sleeping in a lawn-chair out back by the pool.

'A bum, Jared, but he knows Alexander so I haven't called the police to come and haul him away. After all, he just might be a friend. We don't know that much about Alexander yet, do we?'

'No. What's his name, Fred?'

'He didn't give it. He's pretty sloshed, Jared. Not blind-drunk but wobbly-drunk. I thought perhaps Alexander would be back shortly, then *he* could dispose of his friend.'

There was nothing very titillating about that conversation, but after five o'clock when Jared was still sitting there alone in his office, he had the same strong premonition he'd got immediately after talking to Steele.

It annoyed him to be so curious, but finally he went to his apartment, bathed, changed, went downstairs to the dining-room for dinner, and afterwards, with a slightly more virulent wind beginning to blow down out of the north, he started driving towards the Leeds estate.

When he made the swing from the roadway up through the wrought-iron gates towards the distant mansion, he saw that there were lights on in about every room downstairs, and even some light on the second floor. Just for a moment he thought of how the place had glittered when Elizabeth had been alive. Then he drove on around the curving driveway and halted in front of the house.

As he approached the front door several fat raindrops struck. He touched the gong, then stepped back and raised his eyes. It was going to storm again.

The door opened. George half filled it in a tie-less shirt, dark hair uncombed, his bronzed face mephistophelian in the shadows. 'Bad night,' said George. 'Come in.'

Jared was hatless and overcoatless, and, although he too was dressed rather casually, he at least had a tie on. George laid a hand upon his arm. 'How are you about shocks?' he asked. 'Not electrical ones, the other kind.'

Jared looked into the gunmetal blue eyes. 'After surviving your nastiness with old Morgan this morning, I think I can face 'em. Why?'

'It's my father,' said George, and led the way to the entrance archway that opened off the reception room, or entry-hall.

Jared saw Fred Steele with a glass of something transparent in his hand, sitting relaxed near the huge stone fireplace. Nearby was a painfully thin man, tall, bronzed, with black hair and dark eyes, whose head hung and whose face had an unhealthy sheen of perspiration to it.

The shock wasn't very great, actually. Jared had expected, sooner or later, George would find this man. And there was a very marked similarity between them. Of course the elder Alexander's jet-hair was grey-streaked, and his features, once somewhat proud and hawklike, were blurred now from much living, much strife and unpleasantness, and perhaps also from much bafflement.

'Harold Alexander,' said George. 'Care for a drink, lawyer?'

Jared nodded. 'I think I can use one.' He walked over near Steele. 'Is this the man who came around this morning?'

Fred nodded, 'The same. Good thing I didn't call the police. He's a parolee; I don't think the police would have liked it, seeing him like this.'

George turned in the doorway, having heard, and added something else. 'They'd have liked it a lot less, having him turn up at this house about now.' He marched out of the room towards the separate bar-room, without elaborating, but he didn't have to. This rumpled, soiled, husk of a man had once been the husband of the murdered socialite. George was probably making an actual under-statement; the police would have grabbed Harold Alexander swiftly even if he hadn't been drunk.

Fred lit a cigarette, set it scarcely tasted in a huge onyx ashtray and gave Jared a droll look. 'It's a good thing *she* doesn't know. We've had supper and since then we've been drinking and talking. Jared, did you know these Alexanders are part Indian?'

Jared looked quickly at the slumbering drunk. He'd always had some kind of *feeling* about that handsomely bronzed skin, that raven's-wing hair. 'It makes sense,' he replied, sought a chair and dropped down. 'What did this one have to say?'

'Tears,' replied Steele. 'He and George looked at one another, then the stoic-savage-thing came all unstruck. This wobbly one put his head on George's shoulder and cried.'

Jared looked annoyed as he said, 'What's so ridiculous about that?'

Steele's wry expression didn't change. 'Maybe nothing, Jared. But George stood there like he was made of stone, without even speaking. Then he made the old one go get something to eat. It was pretty callous. At least that's how it struck me.'

George returned with a drink for himself and one for Jared. As usual, his martinis were superb. He and Jared exchanged a blank look before George went over to stand behind the chair of his snuffling, unconscious father.

'While I was starting the search, he was already here.'

Jared nodded, sipped and remained silent. He had no explanation coming and didn't particularly want one. He was an attorney, an *estate* attorney, not a father-confessor, and this kind of emotional thing could mean he was going to be sucked deeper into something that he didn't want to be involved in.

'He's been in prison fifteen years. Manslaughter, Jared. Isn't that pretty steep for manslaughter?'

'I'd have to know the details, George. Perhaps it was a light sentence.'

'Tell me something, Jared. Did you know where he was?'

Jared could answer convincingly because he could also answer truthfully. 'No. Your mother never mentioned him. I never asked.'

'But you knew she'd had me, and unlike that Greek goddess who sprang from someone's forehead—'

Jared was on his feet. 'George, I told you I didn't know.' He looked at his wristwatch, his way of intimating a need to be elsewhere very shortly. 'I'm glad you've found him—if you are, George. Otherwise—'

'Sit down,' said Alexander in the identical tone he'd used to old Morgan.

Jared hesitated, but he finally sat. He felt no particular anger now, and that was a mild surprise because he had no more liking for being talked to roughly than anyone else had.

George fished something from a jacket pocket and flung it over. Jared caught it to avoid being struck by whatever it was. Then he held the thing out to examine it. 'A heel,' he said, and put it where Steele could also see it. 'A heel off someone's old shoe.'

George stepped around in front of his father's chair, dropped to one knee and lifted a foot. 'Of *this* old shoe,' he said. 'Care to come match them up?'

Jared didn't move out of his chair so George

42

eased his father's foot back to the floor and straightened up dusting his hands.

Jared had a bad premonition. He raised his eyes to young Alexander. Fred Steele, no longer ironic, was also looking up.

'I found it behind the bulb bed,' explained George. 'There are marks on the stone wall behind the conifers where someone scrambling up the wall tore off his heel.'

They looked stonily at one another for a while, then Jared put the heel upon an end-table and reached for his martini. He drained the glass before saying, 'What else, George?'

'Nothing. Just that heel and the scratch-marks on the wall.'

Fred was thoughtful. 'The police went over the grounds with a fine-tooth comb. If it had been here then ...' Fred frowned.

George turned and gazed at the wasted, dirty figure sleeping in the chair. 'He's got a tumour. I talked with the prison authorities. They put the doctor on the line. A brain tumour.'

Jared dropped his gaze to the perspiring, blank face of the unkempt slumbering stranger. 'Put him in a hospital, George. Have it removed.'

Young Alexander turned, his wide mouth flat and his blue eyes contemptuous. 'Jared, you've always had a practical answer to everything. I remember that from my schooldays. It must be comforting to live in that nice clean, affluent world of yours where

43

everything is either black or white.'

Jared held up the empty glass. 'You make the best martinis I've ever had, George.'

Alexander took the glass but didn't depart with it. 'How do you two like being accessories to murder?'

Steele didn't respond but Jared did—with annoyance. 'What are you talking about! A heel off a man's shoe and some scratches on a stone wall don't prove anything. And I'm no accessory to anything because you're going to turn him over to the authorities, George. If you don't do it, I will.'

The hand holding the glass whitened at the knuckles. George's handsome, brooding face changed in an instant. 'No, you aren't, Jared. He's going to sober up, then he's going to eat well for a few days, shave, bathe, get some decent clothes, and after all that *then* we'll make some decisions. *But not until then!*'

Jared said, 'You can't do that, George. If he's—'

'Who knows about the heel but the four of us? Fred's not going to say anything. Neither are you.'

'I have to,' replied Jared, getting to his feet again. 'Look; you're trying to handle this like it's some kind of private matter, and it isn't, George. But if you'll just use your head, I'll arrange it so that you can have him legally. Did you ever hear of posting bond? Well, that's all it will require. Hell, after all, you studied law;

you know what his rights are as well as I do.'

George still held the empty glass as he looked hard at Jared. 'The law stinks, Jared. I studied it just long enough to know there's nothing more hypocritical on this earth than the law.'

'That's not true. Without the—'

'You listen to me, Jared. There's nothing wrong with *justice*, but people don't get justice in court-rooms, they get the law, and there's a gap between the two a mile wide and a mile deep. He stays here until he's fit to face a court.'

Fred Steele said mildly, 'George, why did you show us the heel off his shoe? If I believed what I think you believe, I'd have burned it. I'd have covered those scratch-marks too. All you've done now is tip your hand; you've put two men who you barely know, at least you don't know *me* very well, in a position where they've just about got to inform against you.'

George said, 'Fred, what would you do for a quarter of a million dollars in cash?'

Steele flushed slowly, looked away then looked back again as he came up to his full height. 'You've made a mistake, George. You've made a misjudgement about me.'

The drowsing man groaned and ground his teeth as though in pain, then he twisted slowly in the chair with both fists clenched. Fresh perspiration popped out on his face.

Jared watched, then said, 'I think we'd better call an ambulance and get him admitted to one of the better hospitals at once. How about Cedars of Lebanon, George?'

Alexander loosened the hold he had on the highball glass. 'If it's the best,' he said, looking down at the slowly writhing man in the chair. 'What are a man's chances when he's fifty or past?'

No one knew but Jared started for the hallway. 'I'll put in the call,' he said.

Over the sick, wasted man in the chair George and Fred Steele gazed steadily at one another for a moment. Fred then said, 'George, did that prison doctor tell you how long he'd had this tumour or how advanced it could be?'

'He didn't know. He said he intended to make X-rays but they are so short-handed up there...'

'Yeah,' muttered Fred, dropping his eyes to the writhing man in the chair. 'You'd better get ready for the worst, George. Then, if that's the wrong attitude, it'll be a wonderful relief for you.'

George leaned over, put aside the highball glass and without looking round said, 'If you were a betting man, Fred, how would you bet—that Jared's calling a private ambulance or a police ambulance?'

Steele's answer was soft. 'I'm not a betting man, sorry.'

CHAPTER SIX

A LIST OF SUSPECTS

It was a private ambulance.

It had only just departed with the sick man, a medical doctor riding with him to administer sedation, when a dark car drove slowly towards the mansion from the street entrance and the three men, George Alexander leading, hadn't quite reached the main living-room when car lights flashed momentarily across the windows, alerting them to this fresh arrival.

Fred Steele stepped to a nearby window, looked, then said, 'Visitors, George. You're lord of the mansion.' Fred shrugged and stepped away from the window. 'Frankly, if no one objects, I'd just as soon retire.'

George was looking at Jared, his expression readable: Had Jared *also* called the police? But George didn't ask the question. Even if he'd intended to, someone's big fist upon the door diverted him. As he went back, Fred said, 'Did you get in touch with the authorities?'

Jared shook his head and two minutes later he was made to look as though he'd prevaricated, because the two large men flanking George when he returned to the main sitting-room, were both policemen. Detective Sergeant Al Hopper and Detective Dan

47

Harlow. As George made the introductions, he looked directly at Jared. Obviously, he believed this was too great a coincidence.

The five of them moved farther into the large sitting-room to chairs and Sergeant Hopper, evidently the spokesman of the police duo, lit a cigarette, glanced around then said, 'I'd like to sort you gentlemen out.' He'd been newly assigned to the Leeds affair and although he'd read all the reports to-date, and was familiar with all the names, he was not familiar with the faces.

Jared took over from there, explaining who he was, who Fred Steele was, and of course who the dead woman's son was. Sergeant Hopper nodded. He could now associate faces with names, he said. Leaning back, smoking serenely, Detective Dan Harlow was a silent shadow of Sergeant Hopper. His eyes moved, his head moved occasionally but he was very quiet.

Hopper said, 'I suppose you know the evidence.' He made a question of it and seemed inclined to address himself mostly to Jared Dexter. 'The victim was strangled by her own hair. The autopsy confirmed that, otherwise it would seem pretty bizarre, wouldn't it?' Hopper's gaze drifted to George Alexander. 'The reason we drove out tonight is because I heard late this afternoon when I returned to headquarters that you had been in, asking questions.'

'True,' nodded George.

'Well, you deserve to be kept current, Mr. Alexander, although you'll appreciate there will be some facts we cannot share.'

George nodded again, his posture slouched, his expression impassive, his eyes watchful. It was Jared who got the conversation back on course. He said, 'Sergeant, in a month the police usually make progress. I know because I have to see that evidence from time to time in my work. Where does the Leeds case stand as of now?'

'We have three suspects,' stated Hopper with candour. 'Three men Mrs. Leeds knew. Men who attended her parties and who moved in her social circle. Two are married, one is not.'

'Names?' asked Jared, and Sergeant Hopper shook his head, which shouldn't have surprised Jared or the others. 'Well then, Sergeant, tell us this. What kind of motivation did these men have?'

'That's not easy to answer either,' said the detective. 'None of them were poor, none have had recent financial reverses, normally I'd say none would have any reason to commit murder. But someone certainly did it, didn't they?'

Jared said, 'Blackmail?'

Hopper shook his head. 'Seems unlikely, but someone did get money. Either an outright grant, or a loan, I'm not sure which.'

'If you don't know that, Sergeant, how do you know this person wasn't blackmailing Mrs. Leeds?'

'I didn't say he wasn't. I said it seems unlikely.'

For a moment the five men sat in silence. Jared, who could have asked the obvious question: if this suspect had got the money after all, why would he have killed Elizabeth Leeds? leaned back to get more comfortable where he sat, and waited for the elaboration he knew would come next. But Hopper didn't speak next, it was Fred Steele.

'Well, well,' he said quietly, near to smiling at the detectives. 'His name wouldn't be Elbert Carling would it?'

Sergeant Hopper studied Steele a moment before answering. 'It would be. And how did you arrive at that, Mr. Steele?'

'Simply enough, Sergeant. I've been almost three weeks trying to create some kind of order out of Mrs. Leeds's private papers. Over the past four months she has withdrawn a great amount of money from her bank accounts, but there was no record of her paying bills with it, or of spending it at all. On the other hand, it wasn't redeposited, nor put in her deposit boxes at the bank. And it wasn't anywhere in the house.'

Hopper murmured, 'Very good, Mr. Steele. Go on.'

Fred looked briefly at George, then at Jared.

'Well, everything else gradually formed a pattern of behaviour, as usually occurs when one makes personal audits. Except this quarter of a million dollars. It had simply vanished without a trace.' Fred paused, then plunged on. 'I found a paragraph in her personal diary. It said Bert Carling got the money he was after.'

Hopper inhaled and exhaled, but when Fred said no more he spoke up. 'Is that all it said? Did it mention Elbert Carling—the writer?'

'No. I've told you all it said. And if I hadn't been very curious, even that entry might not have meant very much.'

'You didn't tell anyone? Mr. Dexter, for instance, or Mr. Alexander?'

'It was too vague for that. I had no intention of mentioning it to anyone until I either found out more, or else discovered that it wasn't really pertinent.'

'It was pertinent all right, gentlemen,' said Sergeant Hopper. 'Elbert Carling, as you probably know, is a very prominent and successful author. Personally, I enjoyed his *Secrets Of A President* very much. It intrigued me because as a policeman, I could appreciate how much digging he'd done to come up with all those juicy facts. As an investigator Carling is very good.'

Up until now George had sat listening. Now, leaning forward, he said, 'What had Carling been digging for lately, Sergeant?'

Hopper thought a moment before answering, and his silent companion, Detective Harlow, crunched out a cigarette in an ashtray and made a slow, careful study of George Alexander.

'If you aren't familiar with Carling's works, Mr. Alexander,' stated Hopper, 'you wouldn't know that his success has been based on exposés. But very good ones; nothing sensational for the sake of sensationalism. Carling has lifted the folk-art of muckraking to the level of Freudian analysis.'

'But it is still muckraking,' said George, and Hopper smiled slightly at him.

'Yes. Well-written, thoroughly authenticated, charmingly edited muckraking.'

'And did he write his exposés only on prominent people, Sergeant?'

'Yes. I'd guess that's what made his books sell like hot cakes, Mr. Alexander.' Hopper, the old professional policeman, easily anticipated Alexander's next question and held up a hand. 'That's right, Mr. Alexander; the next book was to be a thorough exposé of high society ... Mrs. Leeds as prima donna.' Hopper dropped his hand.

Jared, listening carefully, had got ahead of the conversation and had synthesized its results into one word: blackmail. But it was awkward, sitting there with Elizabeth's son, whom Jared knew now was not as insensitive

52

as he liked to appear, taking part in a dissection that was bound to be painful for George, so Jared kept as still as Detective Harlow.

George eased back in the chair again, hooked his long legs one over the other and glanced easily around. Jared avoided his look, so did Fred Steele. Only the two policemen met it head-on. George said, 'Blackmail, Sergeant?'

'It isn't impossible, is it?' replied Hopper. 'But I've never got a conviction in a serious felony case on just circumstantial evidence alone, Mr. Alexander.'

Jared, thinking somewhat slowly and ponderously, was the only person in the room who had actually been very close to Elizabeth Leeds, and actually he hadn't been so close she'd ever confided in him very much, except about her son. And even there, she'd been reticent to the point of telling him only what she wished done about George's education, mode of living, things like that. What few people knew about scintillating Elizabeth Leeds was that she was a secretive person while never appearing to be.

Still, Jared had a distinct advantage over even the two detectives; he had known her intimate friends, had been at her parties and had met, known, and inevitably appraised, her friends. Not the dozens who came and went, but the constant friends; the other very wealthy, serenely assured, dazzling people.

It was out of this coterie that he mentioned

53

additional names to Sergeant Hopper. 'Elbert Carling, Sergeant—and—Richard Bellah—Paul Niarchos.'

Detective Harlow reacted with a swift blink and a stare. Sergeant Hopper simply gazed at Jared and smiled. 'Shots in the dark, Mr. Dexter?'

Jared didn't return the small smile. 'Not exactly, Sergeant; reducing the elements to their basic denominator.'

'Very good,' purred Hopper. 'Mind telling me how?'

'Not at all. Providing you tell me first that it'll be a worthwhile effort.'

Hopper's smile widened slightly; evidently he was a man who enjoyed matching wits. 'It will be,' he replied, 'quite worthwhile.'

'And those are the other two suspects?'

Hopper nodded without speaking, his smile still up, his probing stare honed with sharp interest.

'Richard Bellah is very wealthy. Even before he retired from stock brokerage he was rich. He is also a married womanizer.'

'So far so good,' said Hopper. 'Go on.'

'He is grey-headed but that's not, I think, a true barometer of the man. He golfs, skin-dives, sails his yacht up at Newport, and is a very good tennis player. I know because I've played with him. In other words, Richard Bellah is virile.'

'And capable,' purred Hopper, 'and willing.

But he's also cursed—or blessed, as you wish—with a huge ego. Am I right, Mr. Dexter?'

'Right as rain, Sergeant.'

'Then where does that take us, Mr. Dexter?'

'I suppose we could say it takes us to probably the oldest reason for man-woman violence under the sun, Sergeant. He wanted her and she wouldn't have any part of him.'

Hopper inclined his head ever so slightly. 'But—murder, Mr. Dexter?'

Jared understood the detective's hesitancy and said, 'You people employ psychologists; ask one, Sergeant. I'm only an attorney.'

'I already have, and the answer was affirmative. Providing the ego is thin-skinned and the virility dominant—among other things. But being just a simple cop, I've reduced it to simpler stuff, Mr. Dexter. Would a man who has everything and who believes he is invulnerable and invincible, do something that could completely ruin him, over one frustration?'

'Perhaps,' said George, speaking slowly, 'if he believed himself so invulnerable he couldn't be caught at it.'

Hopper nodded as though he approved of that. 'Time will tell,' he replied. 'Mr. Dexter. Paul Niarchos?'

'Very rich too, as you know, Sergeant,' replied Jared. 'But also interested in a woman *as* a woman. But with Niarchos the difference is more believable than with Bellah. Paul

55

Niarchos has a very definite consciousness of a childhood and early youth spent in the ghettos and gutters of the Old World. And Paul, I can tell you from knowing him, would react more positively to being put down by someone, than would Dick Bellah.'

Sergeant Hopper smiled broadly, very approvingly. 'Too bad you chose the law, Mr. Dexter,' he enthused. 'You have a gift for seeing inside people. Maybe you knew it and maybe you didn't, but Paul Niarchos has bought his way out of two killings of passion in Europe.'

Jared hadn't known that. It shocked him, but in a way it didn't surprise him. He'd known Paul Niarchos for five years, ever since he'd joined the list of Elizabeth Leeds's admirers, and the impression he'd made on Jared had been a faintly evil one. Niarchos, dark and swarthy and black-eyed, drank hard, lived hard, swore hard and played hard.

CHAPTER SEVEN

A FRESH MYSTERY

By the time Sergeant Hopper and his hulking shadow departed it was past midnight. There were no stars, the moon had gone, and it had begun to rain, although no one was aware of this fact until they all went to the front doorway with Hopper and Harlow.

Afterwards, returning to the sitting-room as though the conference hadn't ended, they seemed less tired than baffled. Fred Steele, standing in front of the fireless fireplace facing Jared and George, said, 'Well, *four* suspects. George, you missed your chance. When it comes out later, Hopper isn't going to like it, that you kept the fourth one hidden.'

George said, 'Do you remember what Jared said about some scratch-marks and a heel off an old shoe proving nothing?'

Fred remembered because he nodded his head. 'But the point is—we didn't tell the police about him.'

Jared was gazing at Steele throughout this brief exchange. Then he said, 'He didn't do it, Fred. You saw the man. He was sick and emaciated. It took a *strong man* to strangle Elizabeth Leeds.'

Steele rocked back on his heels in reflection. George, too, seemed to want to think about that, so for a while there was silence.

Jared rose, hid a yawn and afterwards blew out a big sigh. 'I've got to be in court before eleven in the morning to contest a will. I'll be lucky if I even *awaken* by eleven. Fred, care for a lift back to the city?'

'I'm staying here,' said Steele, 'at my host's suggestion. Thanks all the same.' He left the fireplace to stroll slowly out with Jared.

George trailed them, still silent and seemingly morose. When he and Jared shook hands in the alcove by the front door Jared said, 'If you'd like I'll find out who the best specialist is, and send him round.'

'I'd appreciate it,' Alexander replied. 'Send him directly to the hospital. I'll go down there first thing in the morning.'

On the drive back towards the city with rain coming down by the bucket-load, Jared pushed Fred and George out of his mind and concentrated on Richard Bellah and Paul Niarchos. He included Elbert Carling too, but being more familiar with the other two, he tended to linger longest on them.

By the time he reached his stall in the underground garage of the hotel where he kept a suite of rooms, he was deadlocked for a choice of suspects although he was slightly inclined to favour Niarchos. Admittedly, what tipped the scales was that revelation Sergeant Hopper had made about those two murders in Europe.

He went to bed still thinking about them. Not that he disbelieved the detective; he was perfectly willing to believe Niarchos had killed two people in a passion because he had seen that kind of fire in the man's glances several times, but what puzzled him was the question of the man's willingness to kill a woman he wanted so badly. And Jared had seen enough of Niarchos in the presence of Elizabeth Leeds,

58

to know the man really wanted her very much.

He awakened the following morning with a tongue as rough as a used football field, soothed it with an astringent mouthwash, and went through the tedious ablutions he went through every morning, got dressed to the ominous sounds coming from an empty stomach, then went downstairs to the dining-room for breakfast. One of the best arguments in favour of living in hotels over apartment houses was that a bachelor who didn't know the first thing about cooking and who stood in horror of the messy-kitchen aftermaths, was never bothered by those things.

At the office, he asked his staff-assistant, which was an elegant name for the ill-paid law student who did all his law research, to find out who the best brain specialist in New York was.

The name, when it eventually arrived upon his desk through the cool and handsome hands of his sophisticated secretary, Miss Eloise Jorgenson, was Dr. Maurice Spiegelman. Jared located the specialist's office, got hold of him after a brisk skirmish with his secretary, and explained what he wanted. Dr. Spiegelman was, he said, snowed-under with work.

Jared asked what his usual fee for examinations and consultations was, and when Dr. Spiegelman suggested an astronomical figure, Jared, without a moment of hesitation, doubled it. Dr. Speigelman suddenly recalled that there had been a cancellation for this afternoon. He would go to look at Harold Alexander and report back to Jared Dexter.

Otherwise, Jared put in a long morning at court, and when there was no recess for luncheon his stomach made those ominous and audible rumbles again. He wasn't able to placate it until two o'clock. Then, fed, and satisfied with the court's agreeable decision to entertain his motion to study the reasons why his client's motion to set aside an arbitrary Last Will and Testament should be considered, he returned to the office—and found Sergeant Hopper and Detective Harlow sitting in the ante-room, patiently waiting.

Puzzled, he asked them to come into his larger, more impressive private office, offered them chairs then excused himself long enough to call Miss Jorgenson for any messages that might have arrived in his absence. There were two; one from Reginald Morgan at the bank, and one from Fred Steele at the Leeds mansion. He thanked Miss Jorgenson, made notations on a yellow desk-tablet, then swung to face his beefy and seemingly imperturbable visitors.

Sergeant Hopper didn't waste time. 'We need either your permission as executor, or a court order, Mr. Dexter, to turn a police auditor loose on the Leeds financial affairs. If you refuse, we can of course get the court order, but that usually takes so damned long.'

Jared's brows shot up. 'Why would I refuse,

Sergeant? Certainly you have my permission. If you'll just sit tight a moment I'll have my girl type it up.'

'We'd appreciate that,' smiled Hopper, and let Jared get around from behind his desk, across the room and to the door before he added something else. 'Mr. Alexander turned us down.'

Jared, hand on doorknob, slowly faced back into the room. Hopper nodded at him. Harlow, as usual, only looked and said nothing.

'That was his attitude this morning,' stated Hopper. 'I was a little surprised, although now and then we run across people who, with time to think things over, have changes of heart. But in his case, I can't help wondering why.'

Jared couldn't help wondering why also. He stepped away from the door though; after all, executor though he might be, George Alexander was heir, and with the papers transferring the Leeds estate to him in probate, Jared's actual executorship was little more than a formality.

Sergeant Hopper, watching Jared, said, 'Thought I'd better tell you; wouldn't want to get you in trouble with your client. But if you could persuade him to change his mind ...'

Jared returned to the seat behind the desk and looked at the telephone. George would undoubtedly be at the hospital right now. He couldn't call him there. He most certainly couldn't do that with those two detectives sitting there. They'd be interested and before the day was out they'd know about the fourth suspect. Jared fidgeted and Sergeant Hopper noticed that too.

'Aren't you going to call him?' he asked.

'He won't be home right now,' alibi'd Jared, and forced a smile. 'But I'll get hold of him before evening, Sergeant, and do my utmost to get his approval. After all, what is there to hide?'

'You are very right,' smiled Hopper, heaving up out of the chair. 'All we want to know is the dates and amounts of money Mrs. Leeds withdrew, to make up that quarter of a million dollars that Mr. Steele said last night hasn't been accounted for. Then, we do a little file-searching among her friends to find out who made an equivalent deposit.'

Jared saw them out, returned to his office and reached for the telephone. He didn't believe Sergeant Hopper. He couldn't fathom what the man had really wanted, but he didn't believe it was that missing money because all Hopper would have had to do this morning would have been to drive out to the Leeds mansion and ask Fred Steele to show him what he'd already dug up on that money, and without George there to prevent any such revelation, Jared was confident Fred would have complied.

When Fred came to the telephone,

summoned by one of the servants, Jared asked him if George had left any instructions about what the police were to be told, and not told.

Fred's answer was laconic. 'He said at breakfast this morning I was to give out no information of any kind—he emphasized that—*any kind*—without first clearing it through him. Not you, Jared. He made that clear too. Hereafter everything is to be cleared only through him. It's his prerogative, of course, but it struck me as strange after all we had to say among the three of us last night. Not to mention that little awkward business of his getting you and me involved over his father.'

'Where is he now?'

'At the hospital.'

'I'll go over and talk to him,' said Jared, and settled his desk-phone back in its cradle, then for a moment sat there trying to make sense out of something that was too bizarre to make sense.

There seemed to be one explanation. George had either thought of something, or had discovered something that was critical. What it could be Jared had no idea, but neither did he rule out any possibilities, for after all he had learned long ago to have a world of respect for the intelligence of George Alexander.

He rose to depart, saw the scribbled notes on his pad, sank down again and dolorously reached again for the telephone.

Reginald Morgan came on the line already

knowing who was at the other end. He waived greetings and said, 'Jared, that confounded pup has called for a complete audit, and candidly, I take that as an aspersion.'

Jared was placating. 'Not at all, Reginald. It has to do with some money that isn't accounted for among his mother's effects. The police are also probably going to come to see you about that. There is a prevalent feeling that if this money can be located, perhaps so can a murderer. But it has nothing to do with how you or the bank have handled the estate.'

Morgan was mollified. 'I see. Well, I felt you'd know, that's why I called. By the way, how are you getting along with Alexander?'

'Well enough. We sat and talked until past midnight last night.'

'I think,' said old Morgan, speaking thoughtfully, 'after this I'll reach him through you. If that's all right with you, of course.'

Jared, holding up his wristwatch, said, 'As you wish, Reginald,' and rang off, scratched out the notations on the desk-tablet and rose a second time to leave the office.

That time he made it. On the ride down in the lift he returned to pondering the mystery of George Alexander's refusal to co-operate with the police, and it annoyed him.

When he reached the street a taxi was passing. He hailed it, unwilling as a general rule, to drive his own car in the city, and as he gave the name of the hospital and settled back, it occurred to him that perhaps George was wary of the police because of his father.

That train of thought prompted Jared to tell himself severely that he should have told Sergeant Hopper an hour or so ago about the other Alexander, the emaciated one named Harold. But he hadn't, so of course the delay was being continually prolonged, and when he eventually got round to doing it now, Hopper's first question was undoubtedly going to be: 'Mr. Dexter, as an attorney you surely are aware that something like this can be termed withholding evidence.'

He looked at the sky and found it still cluttered by shreds of storm-clouds, but otherwise there was enough blue showing to indicate this most recent shower was past, and that at least was pleasant, because, dirty as the city was, rain making streaks down the grimy walls of buildings only emphasized the lack of cleanliness.

But the hospital was different. Its outer walls were clean, its enormous parking area washed clear of debris, and as the taxi pulled to the front of the place Jared could see through heavy glass doors to where a glistening corridor led away towards other fresh-scrubbed walls and floors.

CHAPTER EIGHT

A DYING MAN

Jared had no difficulty in locating the quarters of Harold Alexander. For one thing he had a private room, and that implied something to the hospital employees, so they directed Jared to his destination without hesitancy. Then too, the crisp and shiny-nosed girl at the third floor desk remembered George Alexander, and that also helped. She pointed out the room and stood gazing at it as Jared walked away.

It had occurred to Jared any number of times that being as good-looking as the younger Alexander was, could indeed be a handicap. It had also, more sardonically, occurred to him that being so handsome could provide a man with some especially marvellous, even breathless, memories.

When he reached the private room and softly knocked, George met him in the doorway looking as morose as he'd looked when Jared had departed the night before. They nodded, and since George offered no verbal greeting, neither did Jared.

Inside, with the door closed, the room was as silent as a tomb although out in the hospital corridor there was endless sound and motion. The elder Alexander looked even darker

66

against the white sheets and pillow-slip. He also looked surprisingly comfortable and serene. His dark glance looked from Jared to his son, enquiringly.

'The attorney,' said George, bringing up a second chair to place beside the other one at bedside. 'Mr. Dexter.'

Jared smiled, tentatively, watching that thin, lined face. 'It's not as bad as it sounds,' he said to the man in the bed. 'There are all kinds of attorneys.'

'Yes,' murmured the man in the bed, 'I know.' His steady black stare bored into Jared. 'There are public defenders and prosecuting attorneys, and it seems to me there are attorneys for just about everything; even for annulling marriages.'

Jared felt the undercurrent and was made uncomfortable by it. 'I'm the estate-attorney,' he explained, trying another little smile and as before getting no response from either the father or the son.

George remained standing but he motioned for Jared to be seated. Jared ignored the gesture and turned from the sick man. 'Will you tell me why you refuse to let the police look at the estate's financial accounts?'

'You've been talking to Fred,' said George.

'Fred, hell, Sergeant Hopper was at my office an hour and a half ago. George, you know perfectly well he can get a court order.'

'But it will take time.'

67

Jared's exasperation made him short. 'What kind of childish logic is this? There is nothing to hide, nothing at all. All of a sudden you are hostile towards the police. It doesn't make sense, George.'

'I'm stalling, Jared. I've got to.'

'Give me one reason why you have to stall?'

George's gunmetal eyes drifted to the bed where the dark face of the emaciated patient was turned towards the younger men. 'There is your reason,' he said.

Jared didn't look. 'Explain,' he said.

'He was there the night she was killed. He told me so this morning but I thought that had to be the case when we were talking, last night. The heel, Jared, and the scratch-marks on the stone fence.'

Jared started to protest, then changed his mind, turned and went closer to the bed. 'Tell me,' he said. 'What happened that night, Mr. Alexander?'

George was nodding at his father. The elder Alexander saw that, of course, but didn't look to Jared as though he would be much influenced by it. He was, Jared, felt, a solitary man, and whatever he'd been like once, as a young man, now he was simply another ex-convict loner. His kind of a man thought in terms of personal well-being and no other way.

'There was a party going on,' he said, finally, and didn't look at either Jared or his son as he spoke. 'I was tired after the long walk ...

68

George asked why I went there. I'll tell you what I told him. To see Betty. Not to touch her and maybe not even to talk to her. Just to see her. You wouldn't understand and it doesn't matter anyway.'

'Mr. Alexander, *did* you see her?'

'No. There is a room attached to the end of the garage. I was in the garden, round at the back, watching all the people through the big windows. I thought I'd see her eventually, but a man came out of that room at the end of the garage and started towards where I was standing. I thought he'd seen me so I stepped back over a flower-bed into the shadows by the rear wall. He kept coming so I scrambled up the wall. Lost my damned heel doing it. That was a bad thing. I can tell you from experience the cops can run a man down with a lot less to go on. Then I walked about half-way back to the city, found an alley and went to sleep there.'

Alexander licked his lips. 'Next day I read what had happened in the papers.' He finally rolled his head to look at Jared. 'I walked down to the docks and got underneath them to be alone. That ended it, I thought, but a couple of weeks later when I was feeling better I thought I'd go back for a last look before heading west. I hung around all one day, then I saw George. No one had to tell me who he was.'

When Alexander seemed unwilling to speak any more his son said, 'He bummed some money, bought some cheap wine, and came back crying like a baby. You know the rest, Jared.'

'Yes, I know the rest. But two things I'd still like to have explained to me, Mr. Alexander.'

'I don't want to talk any more,' said the man in the bed.

Jared ignored that. 'Why did you abandon your wife and baby, Mr. Alexander?'

The bony face swung, the dark eyes got large. 'Abandon hell,' rasped Harold Alexander. 'I didn't abandon them. I couldn't get work so I robbed a liquor store, and got caught. I wrote letters every day. She didn't get them; I didn't think she would. Her parents had the marriage annulled and put the baby with foster-parents. Later, when she re-married, I guess by then she was used to not having him with her. Anyway—'

'All right,' Jared said soothingly. 'That's enough about that. The other question is: Did you ever try to see her again, or find out where George was?'

Harold Alexander closed his eyes tightly and made a little weak motion. 'Get him out of here,' he said huskily. 'Please get him out of here!'

George touched Jared's arm and jerked his head door-ward. They went out into the corridor, closed the door and George said, 'I can answer that second question for you, Jared. He told me this morning he tried many times to see her. She wouldn't answer his calls

70

or his letters, and when he got into trouble again—not just for the manslaughter thing, his latest, but other crimes too—he gradually gave up.' George looked into Jared's eyes. 'Not very pretty is it?'

Jared side-stepped answering by asking another question. 'Did the specialist I sent, Spiegelman, examine him?'

'Yes. Along with three other doctors.'

'And.'

'Too late to try for a removal, Jared.'

Jared watched two grey-haired men stroll by in solemn conversation. Behind them came a pert little nurse with red hair, green eyes, and a sprinkle of freckles across the saddle of her nose. Any other time he'd have watched her out of sight.

'How can they be so damned sure without looking?' he said a bit weakly. 'Don't they have to take X-rays?'

'They took them. This is a very modern hospital, Jared. They take pictures, develop them and have their consultations before the negatives of a regular photograph would dry out.' George put his hands in his pockets, which was a habit of his. 'Spiegelman said they could operate, could remove most of the tumour, but that in his weakened condition the operation alone might kill him. Spiegelman also said it would kill him anyway, because it'd come back, so if he survived the operation the best we could buy him would be another few months of life. Maybe not even that long. Maybe something will rupture inside his skull any day and kill him anyway.'

'So?'

'I chose Spiegelman's last alternative: do nothing, feed him up, take him home in a few days, let him loll around, paddle in the pool if he likes, drink a little, visit with me, and when it hits at least I'll have known him that long.'

Jared had never claimed to be a hard nor an unemotional man, and at this moment his irritation with George dissolved to be replaced with an unpleasant lump just below the throat.

George then said, 'Now you know why I don't want the cops to know anything. Nothing at all, for a while yet. I don't even want them around the house. He's got a natural aversion to cops. I'm not making alibis for him, Jared. He's what he is and I suppose he himself is responsible. But for the time left, I don't want him upset.'

Jared understood. 'All right, I see your point. But, George, Sergeant Hopper is a bloodhound. If you force his hand he's going to make all kinds of trouble. Let me give him the information he wants. It won't point to your father in any case, and I'll do everything I can to keep them away.'

George stood hunched, hands deep in trouser pockets, staring at the floor. From years back Jared knew one thing about this handsome man; he was stubborn. He never relinquished an idea nor a conviction easily. Where he inherited this characteristic wasn't important; what mattered was that it was there in his make-up.

Then George nodded his head. 'Do as you wish,' he said. 'Just remember what I want—peace for a little while.'

Jared offered his hand. They shook, looking into one another's eyes, then Jared left.

Outside, the day was drawing to a blustery close. Jared waited for the taxi he'd summoned, breathing deeply of cold air. It was fresh and invigorating; he needed it very much to clear out the layers of gloom inside his mind. It helped but it did not succeed in doing that entirely.

He went back to the office, put in a call for Sergeant Hopper, failed to find him, and left word for Hopper to call back. Then he went downstairs to the street again, ducked into an exclusive little bar and had two good jolts of rye whisky before returning to his desk for another telephone call.

Dr. Spiegelman's voice sounded mildly annoyed, but he was pleasant. Jared related what George had told him, for verification. Spiegelman was tactful. 'That is approximately correct,' he said. 'As for how long the man has, Mr. Dexter, I don't know. A thing that size can kill him in his sleep some night, or he might live another three or four months.'

'Make a guess, Doctor, and I'll neither

repeat it nor hold you to it.'

'... Something like four or five weeks. Mr. Dexter, it was curable in its initial stages. But don't blame anyone. Headaches everyone gets, and a man like that, one who views pain as something to be borne, is a prime target. He's had it a long time. Drinking can't help, if for no other reason than because he wouldn't take care of himself while he's drinking.'

'I'll see that your cheque is in the mail in the morning, Doctor. I'm obliged.'

'I'm sorry, Mr. Dexter. I'm *always* sorry. Sometimes, just between the two of us, I am also sick of what I have to do and what I have to say. Good-bye.'

Jared put the telephone aside very gently and rocked forward in his chair to lean on the desk staring at the book-lined wall. Aloud he said, 'How could anyone even imagine such a mess, let alone be part of it? Hopper isn't going to stay away any five or six weeks.'

As though on cue the telephone rang. It was Sergeant Hopper sounding pleasant and half-smiling the way he always seemed to be. Jared said, 'Okay, Sergeant, I've got permission for you to look at the financial statements. But Mr. Alexander has instructed the bank to make an audit and if you wait a few days, you won't need a police auditor at all.'

Hopper made a humming sound, then said, 'How long is a few days, Mr. Dexter; two weeks, three weeks?'

74

'I would imagine the auditors could be finished in three or four days. After all, the bank keeps its audits pretty damned current.'

'Okay, Mr. Dexter, I'll be in your office in three days. Will you get the copy for me and keep it there?'

'Yes.'

After ringing off from this call, Jared rested his head in his hands for a few minutes, then decided to go home. It was beginning to look murky beyond the window anyway.

CHAPTER NINE

LETTERS OF A GHOST

Old Morgan telephoned two days later to say the bank had succeeded in bringing the Leeds Estate audit up to date. But Morgan also said it wasn't an in-depth audit, which would have taken much longer. He wanted Jared to explain this to young Alexander, and also to tell him that if he wished for a more penetrating analysis of the estate it would be prepared at his request.

Jared sat in thought after that conversation speculating on the advisability of keeping up this charade of him acting as some kind of armistice commission between old Morgan and George Alexander.

The only conclusion he arrived at was that at least for the time being he would comply. Then he telephoned Sergeant Hopper.

That afternoon he had to make an appearance in court, so would not be on hand until the following morning, as he told Hopper. The detective decided not to come round to look at the audit until Jared could be there to go over it with him.

That evening, pleased over the outcome of his court appearance, he left the office early, had a light dinner on the way, and drove to the Leeds mansion. The next day would make the third day since he'd heard from George Alexander, and although Fred Steele had telephoned when Jared wasn't in, to say he was getting close to the end of his work at Hyde Park, they had not personally chatted in about the same length of time.

He was reasonably certain George would have his father at home by now, and he was correct. When he drove up to the front of the house, the dark and wizened figure of Harold Alexander appeared at an upstairs window, looking out. Jared waved but Harold Alexander did not wave back.

George was out at the back with the gardener. Jared walked on back and was met by the gardener's craggy smile and by George's brooding look. As Elizabeth Leeds's private attorney and to some extent her trouble-shooter and estate overseer, Jared was well

76

known to all the hired help. He had never been able to pierce the Scottish reserve of the gardener, and had been quite content to leave their relationship that way. They were friends, as now, but that was all.

The man was tactful. Whatever he had been discussing with George, he was perfectly willing to see relegated to second place. He touched his cap to them both, turned and walked off in the direction of the bulb-bed.

George, gazing after him, said, 'Odd thing about people, Jared—the ones you meet in life and truly remember, don't ever seem to be the important people.' He turned back, and smiled. 'Getting philosophical in my dotage. What's on your mind? Had supper?'

They started towards the house side-by-side as Jared said he had, in fact, eaten only a short while ago, and asked about George's father.

'He seems content,' mused George. 'Not happy. I think he lost the ability to be happy a long time ago. But he eats well, drinks a little, bathes, and dresses in clean clothing—to him those seem to be the luxuries. That, and the feeling that no one is going to jump out at him and flash a badge, have made him a lot quieter, more sociable. He even jokes a little with Fred.'

They reached the door to the glassed-in conservatory. Jared, reaching to open it and admit his host first, said, 'Hopper'll be around in the morning to see the audit Morgan has worked up. It's not an in-depth study—that

77

would take weeks—but it'll probably be ample. All Hopper wants to know, I think, is that no one killed Mrs. Leeds because they were bilking the estate and she discovered it. Something like that.'

George paused in the conservatory to cast a sceptical look at Jared. 'How would she have known if that were true? I've been going over Fred's work. She even paid some bills two and three times over. If she had no idea how to manage something as inconsequential as her personal affairs, what makes anyone think she'd have been able to uncover a plot to rob the estate?'

It was a good point. Perhaps more to the crux of it, Jared, who had known her better even than her own son, who had just made this unflattering comment, also knew how glaringly correct her son was.

But all he said to George was: 'Don't query me; see Sergeant Hopper.'

They passed on through to a mahogany-panelled study with books and brass lamps and exposed rafters that made the place seem like a sophisticated monk's cell—an atmosphere which had doubtless been contrived—and Fred was there, standing by a window, cigarette in one hand, cup of coffee in the other. He turned, nodded and said, 'Good to see you again, Jared.' Beyond his wide shoulders the night was nearly down by this time. Beyond the window stars faintly

78

flickered. Fred strode towards a cluttered large table where a lamp burned. 'Won't be long now. Maybe by the end of next week, and you'll be able to sit back and get a pretty fair insight into things.'

'But not murder,' put in George Alexander, and turned as a servant discreetly cleared his throat in the doorway. 'Yes?'

'The cook was wondering, sir, if Mr. Dexter would be here for dinner?'

George didn't ask Jared, he simply said, 'Yes, he will, and if you will, you can bring us some drinks in here.'

Jared had eaten, not heavily but adequately. He wasn't hungry. He *could,* however, use the drink. It didn't occur to him to speculate upon the merit of perfect servants until the tray came with his favourite, a martini, plus a somewhat massive scotch-and-soda for George, and a whisky-and-water for Fred Steele. Not that the servant hadn't had ample time by now to know everyone's preference, but it still was nice to think that there were still competent servants in the world.

'We'll have a visitor after dinner,' said George, holding his glass up. 'Elbert Carling.' At Jared's quick look and Fred's expression of ironic interest, George explained. 'He called twice today. I stalled him this morning. This afternoon I told him to come along. He wants to discuss Elizabeth.'

Jared said tartly, 'The hell with him. You

don't have to put up with this, George.'

Alexander smiled slightly. 'I know that. But I'm as curious about him as he doubtless is about me.'

'If he's really writing some damned book about the social giants, then you can bet your boots he won't be very flattering to you in it.'

'I've surmised that too,' said Alexander. 'But as I said a while ago—there is still a murder to be resolved.'

Fred Steele went to a chair, sat and crossed his legs. He was a listener and a watcher, evidently, because he sipped his drink and said nothing.

Jared was hostile to the idea of Elbert Carling. He had never cared much for the man. Carling, despite his wealth, had always managed to put Jared in mind of a lean vulture.

'It's your ball game,' he told George, and went to the window to stand gazing out into the night. 'Just be careful what you say.'

George smiled over that. 'I am, occasionally.' Then he dismissed that subject and moved to another one. 'Jared, how well did you know David Leeds?'

It was an unexpected subject, and touched upon something Jared had to face his interrogator to answer. 'Not very well. He died a couple of years after I took the job of minding Mrs. Leeds's legal affairs.'

'Did you know he and Paul Niarchos were involved in some kind of business venture together?'

Jared hadn't known that, and it surprised him. He looked over to find Fred Steele showing that enigmatic little ironic smile of his. 'No,' he said, 'I didn't know it. And if it's true, how did *you* find it out?'

Fred Steele finally spoke. In a casual way he said, 'I'm at fault, Jared. There were several references among some old letters I located of Mrs. Leeds's. Nothing that gave any specifics.' Steele rose, ambled to the laden table and searched through a pile of papers. 'It's a bit of a mystery, actually,' he said, sifting out several pieces of letter-paper and handing them to Jared. 'The bank has no records of any transactions involving David Leeds and Paul Niarchos, and that makes me assume their deals were out-of-pocket affairs; whether in order to avoid some income tax annoyances, or simply because it was so long ago, and possibly so unprofitable a partnership that David Leeds never showed them in his records, is anyone's guess.'

All the letters said was that David Leeds had flown to Europe to meet Paul Niarchos in Paris for a business conference, and also, in another letter addressed to Elizabeth and written in the hand of David Leeds, that the partnership was beginning to show some promise although it was too early as yet to explain. The last letter had a notation on the margin in Elizabeth's handwriting to the effect that she had received as a gift from her husband, a beautiful cameo brooch set in engraved white gold, 'from their own supply.'

Jared finished reading, put the letters back on the desk and looked at Fred. 'Nothing in the records here?'

Steele shook his head. 'I made a thorough search, but as a matter of fact I didn't really expect to find anything. After all,' he gestured towards the table, 'this is all pretty much personal stuff.' Steele looked at Jared. 'We wondered if you remembered hearing anything, or if you'd seen anything that might refer to gold, white or otherwise, in any of the income tax forms, or in the audit returns by the bank.'

Jared shook his head, thinking back. He'd have remembered, he was confident of that, because, aside from being zealous in the performance of his legal duties, the Leeds estate had been for many years his sole source of support; he had been very careful of it.

Fred returned to his chair. 'Probably nothing,' he said, reseated himself and crossed his legs again.

George was less sanguine. 'Fred may be correct, Jared, but Niarchos is a suspect and there has been a murder. One way or another the thing should be brought out into the open.'

The servant came to summon them to dinner.

Jared was quiet at the table. His brief few

meetings with David Leeds had left him with a distant and vague impression of the man. Leeds had been a taciturn, rather introspective person, tall and with quick, hard blue eyes. Since he listened rather than talked, it had been hard to make any assessments respecting the man. As a young man, Jared had feared him; after his death Jared had remembered him simply as a financial genius with whom he'd never been able to establish a *rapport*. The only feeling he could honestly recall was one of relief that the man had died.

George broke across these thoughts to say, 'You're not eating, Jared.'

'I had dinner in the city before coming out. I told you that.'

'Then how about another drink?'

Jared shook his head. He'd got all the pick-me-up that he'd needed from that drink in the study. George smiled across the table at him.

'Paul Niarchos . . . ?'

Jared returned the smile, but very slightly. 'Yes. *And* David Leeds.'

'So tomorrow you'll go see old Morgan and see what can be dug up.'

'Maybe but not necessarily. I've got the estate records in my office too. I'll look through them.' Jared looked at Fred. 'It might not be a bad idea for you to do some more digging out here.'

'Already have,' replied Steele. 'From one end of the place to the other end. And there are only those letters.' Fred's gaze lifted. 'I don't see how it could have amounted to much anyway, Jared. If it had, Leeds couldn't have avoided leaving some record. And if it's necessary, of course we can make a minute audit—how much dividend each investment paid against how much money he had—and if more money turns up than was earned, Leeds probably got it from another source. But proving it came from some elusive partnership with Niarchos of which there seem to be no records ...' Fred shrugged his big shoulders and returned to his meal.

Ten minutes later, just as they were finishing, a servant came to announce the arrival of Mr. Elbert Carling. He had been shown into the main salon, the servant said, with somewhat of an air reminiscent of the days when Elizabeth used words like 'salon' instead of sitting-room, which the three men at the table would have preferred.

George rose first. He leaned upon the table like a field-marshal giving final orders, and said, 'As you said, Jared, it's my ball-game. Okay?'

Jared and Fred rose nodding.

CHAPTER TEN

A SHOCKER

Elbert Carling did not look like a muckraker. At least his attire was beyond reproach and his manners were suave, pleasant, seemingly second-nature. It was in his tawny-tan eyes, the slightly elongated and narrow cast of his features, the small tightness of his mouth, that one might find some reason to be suspicious of the man.

He knew Jared and smilingly acknowledged his presence, but the interest he displayed in Fred Steele was second only to his quick, sharp study of George Alexander as the four of them took seats in the major living-room.

He said, as his opening gambit, that it was kind of George to see him. George's reply was predictably blunt and to the point.

'I'm interested in your work,' he said. 'Someone told me you are now at work on something touching upon Mrs. Leeds.'

Carling smiled gently, as though humouring a child, and answered in a well-modulated voice. 'Well, it *is* my livelihood, Mr. Alexander. As far as Mrs. Leeds was concerned, it would be impossible to write a factual account of the genuine Ivory Tower People—not the jet-set, the *genuinely* patrician set—without mentioning her.'

Jared, watching Carling, thought of that notation in the dead woman's diary saying this man had got some money. He was trying to imagine, looking at Carling, listening to him, what that money had bought.

George startled Jared by his second remark to Carling. It was made in the identical quiet calm tone of voice he'd used in threatening Reginald Morgan. Only this time it was prefaced by something else.

'Would you care for a drink, Mr. Carling? It might be the only one we ever share. If you do your exposé in a way that reflects on either Mrs. Leeds or me, I'll break your back.'

Fred had never heard George speak like this, evidently, because he looked only a shade less startled than did Elbert Carling.

Jared sought for something to say quickly but nothing came to mind, and in the interim Carling's thin face reddened. He glared and shot an answer back. 'Mr. Alexander, if you have nothing to worry about, then there can't be much to fear, can there?'

'That's a silly remark,' retorted George. 'People do things to other people, Mr. Carling. What my parents did to me doesn't reflect to anyone's credit, mine included. A muckraker could make it look pretty questionable that I was even legitimate. After all, Mrs. Leeds *did* keep me out on the West Coast, didn't she? How much of a writer would you have to be to get all kinds of insinuations into that story?'

Carling was listening closely, but Jared saw that the man was making a clinical study of George too. There was one thing Jared was sure of: Elbert Carling would make a vindictive and dangerous enemy, and George had just given him good reason for a fine, first-class antagonism.

'I've been threatened before,' said Carling, relaxing against the back of his chair. 'It doesn't intimidate me in the least.'

George smiled. 'Care for that drink, Mr. Carling?'

They looked directly at one another for the length of time it took for Carling to decide he'd go along with George's initiative in their meeting, and nod his head. 'That would be gracious of you, Mr. Alexander. Whisky-sour?'

George rose and walked off in the direction of the separate bar-room. The moment he'd passed from sight Carling turned a cold smile upon Jared. 'What have we here, Dexter?' he asked. 'The man doesn't look much like his mother and he most certainly doesn't act like her. What is your opinion?'

'I don't have any,' replied Jared, being very careful.

It was Fred Steele, smoking and looking calmly amused, who gave part of an answer to the writer's question. 'If I were in your boots, Mr. Carling, I'd assume he didn't make bluffs.'

'Would you indeed, Mr. Steele?' Carling reached inside his coat, drew forth a beautiful, hammered silver cigarette case and lit up. The cigarette was evidently of Turkish or Balkan manufacture because its smell was altogether different from the aroma of American cigarettes. As he tucked the case away again, Carling gave his attention to Jared again.

'Why does he refer to her as Mrs. Leeds, instead of as his mother?'

'Ask him,' grunted Jared. 'After all, he barely even knew her.'

'And her murder—what does he think of that?'

Jared repeated what he'd said earlier. 'Ask him.'

George returned with the mixed drink, handed it to Carling and returned to his chair. As he sat down he said, 'If it's possible for us to be acquaintances, Mr. Carling, I'll do my share. If it's not, then I'll also do my share.'

Carling held the drink without raising it and said, 'Another threat. Mr. Alexander, you are wasting your time.' He considered the glass, then deliberately made a show of setting it aside without touching it. As he straightened up again, George gave that rather chilly smile again, and spoke.

'I don't make threats, Mr. Carling. I make promises. There's a difference. It's the same as the difference between saying something and doing it.'

Carling leaned as though to rise. 'Anything else?' he murmured.

'One more thing,' said George. 'Why did Mrs. Leeds pay you off?'

Carling hung on the edge of his chair as though he'd been unexpectedly slapped. Jared saw Fred Steele crush his cigarette in an ashtray from the corner of his eye, but otherwise he was watching Carling. The man looked paler than before.

Then he said, 'She didn't.'

George shot back an answer. 'You're a liar—Mr. Carling. Care to think it over and try again?'

'I am *not* a liar and I'm not going to sit here and listen to these—'

'You're not going to leave until you answer.'

Jared squirmed. He didn't believe George would actually become violent, but he disapproved strongly of his behaviour. But before he could intercede with a verbal protest, Carling was speaking again.

'I don't know what your source is, Mr. Dexter, but I can assure you it is incorrect.'

George sat there shaking his head. 'Once more. This time try the truth.'

Carling, still perched forward in his chair, looked steadily at George for a bit, then slowly turned his head. 'Dexter, is this your work?'

Jared hesitated over his reply. He did not like Elbert Carling, but George's behaviour left him with a bad feeling in that direction too. He shook his head without answering and turned towards young Alexander.

'You're not going about this right,' he said.

George was silent until he'd pulled a scrap of paper from a pocket. Then he said, 'My ball-game, Jared; remember?' And as he raised the slip of paper he looked directly at Carling. 'Thirty thousand dollars. Does that jar your memory? No? Well, it was given you by personal cheque over a year ago by Mrs. Leeds, and in case you want to say you never saw any such cheque, it was deposited to your account at your bank the same day she wrote it for you.'

Jared was dumbfounded. If he hadn't been, and had turned his head, he would have seen an odd expression of surprise and chagrin cross Frederick Steele's features. But it was Elbert Carling whose face turned white.

George pushed the slip of paper back into a jacket pocket. 'You're not only a liar, Mr. Carling, but you are a damned poor one.'

There was enough tension in the big room to cut with a knife. For some little while no one had anything to say. Obviously now, George hadn't been bluffing. Jared assumed, and thought Carling must be assuming the same thing, that if George hadn't been bluffing about the money, he wasn't bluffing about the threats either.

Carling finally said in a raspy voice, 'It wasn't blackmail, Mr. Alexander, regardless of what you think.'

90

No one moved or spoke. Carling had some explaining to do and no one was going to help him. He didn't drop his eyes before George Alexander's steady gunmetal stare, and perhaps that was at least in his favour.

'She paid me thirty thousand dollars to use my contacts to ascertain whether her husband and Paul Niarchos had ever dissolved some partnership she said they'd had years ago. I was the only person she knew, she said, who could handle that for her without blundering. At first I suggested that she employ private investigators. She was afraid Paul would find out. It was a reasonable fear, Paul Niarchos *is* something of a cloak-and-dagger man. She then doubled her original offer of fifteen thousand for my services, and I agreed to do as she wished.'

George motioned towards Carling's untouched glass. 'Tonic for the nerves,' he said. 'Why didn't you say all this in the first place, Mr. Carling?'

The writer gulped the drink before answering. 'Because no one alive knew anything about this but me. Mrs. Leeds is dead.'

'That's not much of a reason,' said George. 'What is the rest of it?'

As Carling floundered Jared decided on a gamble and said, 'Paul Niarchos?'

Carling nodded. 'Jared, you know the man. He killed two people in Europe. He has great wealth and is absolutely unscrupulous. That kind of man wouldn't hesitate to use violence again. Or to hire it. I had no intention of ever saying a word about what I did for Elizabeth again.'

George, unworried about Niarchos, said, 'Mr. Carling, what did you discover to earn your thirty thousand dollars?'

Carling shook his head vigorously. 'I'll give the money back to her estate.'

Young Alexander sighed and looked drolly at Jared. 'Do you suppose Sergeant Hopper could make an arrest for suspicion of blackmail, if I signed a complaint against Carling?'

Jared didn't answer because, obviously, he wasn't supposed to. *This* time the threat sounded very real. He and George and Fred turned to gaze at Carling. The man's self-assurance had deserted him. Perhaps the drink had helped, but even so Carling looked badly upset.

Finally, he said, 'There are four of us in this room. Any one of you could telephone Paul Niarchos five minutes after I've left—if I told you what I did to earn that thirty thousand dollars.'

'And if you *don't* tell us,' said George, 'you aren't going to leave this room. Not for a long time, anyway, and you probably won't look the same either. Mr. Carling, you're between a stone and a hard place, and I don't feel the least

92

bit sorry for you. Now either speak up or stand up!'

Carling turned in obvious appeal to Jared, but it was heretofore silent Fred Steele who said, 'No one is going to telephone Mr. Niarchos, Carling. Excepting Jared, none of us even know the man. And Jared works for the Leeds estate. If you had to pick three men to confide in, I don't think you could do much better ... The alternative being what it is. I'd advise you to speak up.'

Carling did. 'Paul got David Leeds interested in funding an international syndicate that dealt in dental gold.'

Jared looked at Carling as though the man were mad. 'Dental gold,' he blurted out. 'Carling, David Leeds was a multi-millionaire. He didn't play for peanuts.'

'Let me finish, Jared. This was *not* peanuts. Have you heard of the German death factories during World War Two? Well, that is where the dental gold came from, and out of something like six million mouths came more gold than has been produced by most of the gold mines on earth. It was already refined gold, Jared. Pure enough to be melted into ingots. Paul Niarchos made the contact. I never learned how. I didn't actually try very hard to learn about that aspect of the business. David Leeds helped fund the enterprise.'

Fred Steele lit another cigarette and frowned. His accountant's mind was working.

'Leeds couldn't hide that kind of income. What happened to the gold, and to the profit he and Niarchos had to make?'

Carling didn't know. He had, he told them, reported verbally to Elizabeth what he had found out. He made her swear a solemn oath never in any circumstances to tell either her husband or Paul Niarchos, what he had told her. She had promised.

George asked a pregnant question. 'How long was that before she was murdered, Mr. Carling?'

'Five years; perhaps six years, I'm a bit hazy when that much time passes.'

Jared looked over at George and said, 'More to the point, how long was all this before *David Leeds* died?'

Carling nodded his head. 'One year, Jared, and what you are thinking has haunted me ever since. *Now* do you understand why I'd have done anything to keep from having to tell about it?'

CHAPTER ELEVEN

A CLIMAX TO TROUBLE

The following morning, very early, Jared returned to the Leeds mansion for breakfast. It had been agreed after Carling's revelation of the night before, for the four of them to hold a conference. Jared still did not like Carling, and although he hadn't quite decided whether he trusted the man or not, he had still fought George the night before to include Carling in this meeting for breakfast.

But his objective was nothing more than to let Carling know exactly what it was decided to do about what he'd told them. Otherwise, if they *did* decide to bring in the police, and hadn't told Carling, they would have broken their promises to him; at least their implied promises.

In Jared's opinion there was no question at all about telling Sergeant Hopper, and that was the main reason he'd insisted that the breakfast meeting be held early—because Hopper was coming to Jared's office later in the morning.

When George admitted him to the house he saw Fred with a cup of coffee and a cigarette, crossing from the study towards the living-room, where lights burned. He could also detect a faint aroma of breakfast. It made him hungry.

George didn't smile when he greeted Jared. He didn't speak except for the greeting, until they joined Fred in the large living-room they'd used the night before. Then he said, 'I'm afraid we will have to eat without Mr. Carling. Last night after he left us he went to his residence, packed two bags, taxied to the international airport and took the first available flight out—to London.'

Fred, standing near the fireplace, nodded over his host's shoulder at Jared. He seemed a lot less chagrined about this development than George did. In fact, Fred still gave Jared the impression of an ironically amused bystander. He said a little sardonically, 'If you two are worried about points of honour, remember that last night although there may have been *implications* about keeping Carling's secret, none of us gave his word.'

George turned, annoyed. 'I didn't imply anything at all like that, Fred. I had no intention of doing so right from the start. We're after a murderer, not State secrets.'

A servant announced breakfast. As they went to the table, where lights burned to dispel the dawn gloom, and were seated, Jared asked the question which had been bothering him since last night.

'George, how did you find out Mrs. Leeds had given thirty thousand dollars to Carling?'

'I thought I made that plain last night,' came the reply. 'I went to the bank—her bank first—and spent all the morning going over old accounts. When I found the withdrawal I then went to *his* bank and matched it among his records of deposits. As for *how* I did it, there was no difficulty at *our* bank, and it cost me, to be frank, two thousand in cash, to be left alone in a small room with Carling's records.'

Jared drank his coffee, looked at Fred and

smiled a little thinly. He didn't say anything. He didn't have to.

George ate for a moment then spoke again. 'Jared, what is the next move?'

Jared had an answer ready. 'Sergeant Hopper. What is the alternative?'

'Paul Niarchos,' said George, and both his companions stared. He either didn't see their looks or chose to ignore them. 'That's a terrible way for anyone to die—strangled to death. But for a woman who couldn't fight back...'

Jared slowly put aside his knife and fork. 'George, I allowed one mistake to compound itself. Your father. I'll be damned if I'll be party to anything like you're suggesting now. And while we're on the subject of physical violence, you acted like a fool last night with Carling.'

Alexander's head came up, his gaze lingered on Jared's face. 'Tell me,' he said calmly, 'would we have got that information from him otherwise? No, we wouldn't have, Jared, and for your information, during the past couple of days when you were busy, I was also busy. For example, in going back through Carling's past I discovered something: He didn't fear courts nor lawsuits; he'd gone the limit with both. It was part of the hazards of his business and he kept some very good attorneys, but there *was* something he dreaded—physical violence. So, I used it. Now I'll ask you again—if I hadn't known this, and if it hadn't been made clear to him last night that it was going to happen, what would we have to discuss this morning?'

Fred smiled at Jared. 'It's the truth.'

Jared returned to his breakfast and afterwards finished the coffee before speaking. 'You used the same approach with old Morgan at the bank. Don't tell me you'd also discovered that he—'

'You know damned well,' growled George, 'he had that coming. You were there throughout the meeting between us. He started out to dominate, to bully, and I've never been passive towards bullies, not since I was a lonely little kid in school. Forget Morgan. Forget these absurd ethics for a while, Jared. Maybe next year we can sit on my verandah overlooking Santa Barbara and the ocean, have a highball and reminisce, but that's next year. *This* year we want a murderer.'

Jared shrugged. 'Hopper is coming to my office for the audit-copy this morning, later on. I'll tell him what Carling said. All right?'

George nodded. 'You can also tell him that unless he hauls Paul Niarchos in within a couple of days—'

Jared interrupted. 'Don't say that, George. I'll tell you right now that I'm not going to be party to any more of these threats, or any violence either.'

The servant reappeared to refill their cups, then softly to depart. Outside, dawn was turning the wet, chilly world an uninviting corpse-grey colour. The dining-room lights contrasted strangely with that other, rather dismal and unpleasant brightness. Jared's mood came closer to matching what lay outside, than what was inside.

Fred leaned back and lit a cigarette. He tossed the pack on the table as though inviting the others to join him. Neither of them did; George Alexander didn't smoke at all, and while Jared Dexter once had, he did not smoke now.

There was something else to discuss and George brought it up. 'If Carling, in some wild attempt to save his neck, telephoned Niarchos last night before he left for London, Hopper isn't likely to have a very easy job of making the arrest.'

Jared was sanguine about that. 'He won't have an easy time of it whether Carling telephoned the man or not. Paul Niarchos, as I presume is the case with Carling, keeps some high-powered legal lights on his payroll on an annual retainer basis. Even if Hopper can make the arrest, Niarchos will be out on bail thirty minutes after he's taken in and booked. And there's something else, George, you might want to consider. What proof will Hopper have? Your word, my word, and Fred's word, that Carling implicated Niarchos in some kind of business deal with David Leeds—who is dead. Maybe the business deal was a grisly, disgusting affair; so far not even Carling has been able to say there was anything illegal about it.'

'But if we assume Niarchos discovered that Mrs. Leeds found out he'd somehow bilked her husband . . . ?'

Jared was shaking his head before George ceased speaking. 'Pure theory, George. So much smoke in the wind. To make an arrest Hopper will need a damned sight more than our speculations.'

Jared put aside his napkin, glanced at his wrist and rose. He actually had a couple of hours before Sergeant Hopper would appear at the office, but he'd said, and heard, all he wanted to at this latest meeting. 'I've got to be getting along.'

The three of them went out to the front of the house together. As Jared slid behind the wheel of his car George smiled down at him. 'Don't be too indignant, Jared. I'm not going to attack anyone. Unless of course I'm attacked first. But as a façade you'll have to admit that this far it has worked very well.'

Jared drove off with an annoyed light in his eyes. Fred had stood back there wearing that ironic smile of his, and George had been smiling in what Jared had to describe as a superior and condescending manner. It was annoying. Also, it irritated him to think that they hadn't called Hopper last night after midnight, when Carling had still been handy.

His conclusion was that they had all acted like amateur detectives. The sole mitigating circumstance had been the way George had run down that thirty thousand dollars so neatly.

When he arrived at the office Miss Jorgenson was already at work typing alterations in a brief he'd recently submitted in court and which had been unacceptable as he'd offered it. She smiled and he smiled, but for him at least it was an effort.

Half an hour later, much earlier than Jared expected, Sergeant Hopper arrived. He was alone, which was the first time Jared had ever seen him without Detective Harlow filling in as his shadow.

Jared got the bank-audit and passed it over. Hopper's good-nature seemed predominant this morning. He sat a moment looking through the pages, then he put the audit into an inside pocket and said, 'You've been busy, Mr. Dexter.' Hopper's blue eyes were almost gay, but they also were piercing. They gave Jared a sudden idea and it left him flustered and just a little breathless: *Of course!—Sergeant Hopper'd had him watched!*

He could feel the guilt-stain spreading up across his face and couldn't control it. He got angry, but one second of reflection showed that to be a luxury he could not afford, so he nodded his head and waited for Hopper to speak again.

'Meetings at the Leeds place until the wee hours of the morning, then back again for more meetings only three or four hours later.' Hopper was still looking as pleasant as though they were discussing what a nice day it was going to be now that the rain had departed. 'And of course there is Harold. . . .'

Jared felt like swearing at Hopper. The detective's smile put his nerves on edge. 'What's wrong with meetings, and with old Harold Alexander, Sergeant? After all, the Leeds estate *is* my client.'

Hopper said, 'No need to be so defensive, Mr. Dexter. As for Harold—I take my hat off to his son; without any reason I can find—and believe me, I've investigated—he's taken his father in, to die.'

'You're thorough,' admitted Jared, grudgingly, and breathed an inward sigh because Hopper hadn't mentioned a possible connection between Harold Alexander and his late ex-wife's death.

Hopper didn't seem to consider that much of a compliment. 'It was nothing, really. A few telephone calls. I'm sorry about the elder Alexander's condition.' Hopper yawned. 'A bit early, isn't it? I talked to Dr. Spiegelman last night. Got his name from the hospital. Looks like poor George Alexander is one of those tough-luck people, doesn't it?'

Jared nodded. 'Sergeant, you're not sitting there just to bemoan the inevitable fate of a dying man. What else is on your mind?'

'A couple of things. Carling, for example.

But we'll come back to him later. I've got a tail on him too, only he's turning out to be a lot more wide-ranging than you and the others were.'

'What others?'

'George Alexander, of course, and Fred Steele. They'll do to answer your question for now, Mr. Dexter.' Hopper drew forth a two-page typewritten report of some kind and gazed thoughtfully at it. 'I've got something here that might interest you. A coroner's exhumation report.'

Jared was jarred. 'Exhumation report—on whom? Sergeant, if you've exhumed Mrs. Leeds without the express permission of the estate, you are in for some—'

'Not so fast, Mr. Dexter. It was *Mister* Leeds, not *Mrs.* Leeds, and I got the court order three days ago, so it was perfectly legal.'

Jared was dumbfounded. '*David* Leeds?'

Sergeant Hopper didn't answer, instead he glanced at the papers in his hand as he said, 'Mr. Leeds, poor devil, didn't die of the coronary thrombosis that is shown on the Death Certificate of his doctor, although it was a perfectly pardonable conclusion without a lot of fancy pathology to make absolutely certain. *David Leeds was strangled to death.*'

The telephone rang. Jared, staring at Sergeant Hopper, didn't even reach for it until Hopper pointed to the thing. Then he lifted it only long enough to say, 'Miss Jorgenson, take

103

it down, and I don't want to be disturbed until Mr. Hopper leaves. Thank you.'

CHAPTER TWELVE

NO END TO SURPRISES

Sergeant Hopper's visit, presumably to take no more than perhaps half an hour while he and Jared Dexter discussed the bank-audit, stretched until noon, and they even went to luncheon together.

Sergeant Hopper's reaction to Carling's story was not astonishment, as Jared expected, but then Sergeant Hopper was a lifelong policeman, he did not react with astonishment very often.

Nor, as he said over lunch, was he going to rush round and arrest Paul Niarchos. 'I'm only three years away from retirement, Mr. Dexter; all I need is for someone like Niarchos to sue the Department over something I did.' He smiled at Jared. 'But if there is *proof*, believe me, I don't care where he goes, I'll get him.'

That, of course, was the problem: proof. Proof of what? Murder, some kind of illegality involving dental gold? Jared said, 'If Niarchos finds out what Carling did for Mrs. Leeds, or if he finds out what Carling said about him ...' Jared dolorously wagged his head.

But Sergeant Hopper only shrugged. 'If I were a guessing man, Mr. Dexter, I'd hazard a guess that if Niarchos killed Mrs. Leeds, that was why—because he *did* know something.'

'He could have been in love with her. It was pretty obvious what he wanted, Sergeant.'

Hopper made a little gesture of scepticism. 'Mr. Dexter, love or no love, Niarchos wouldn't be the first man to choose survival, over love for a beautiful woman.'

Jared knew Paul Niarchos and had no difficulty now in believing Hopper could be quite right. But had Elizabeth voluntarily told Paul Niarchos whatever it was that had inflamed him so much that he killed her? It was hard to believe; Elizabeth also knew Niarchos, and as it might turn out, she could have known him even better than Jared, and if this were so, she certainly wouldn't have done something she suspected might result in her own death.

Suddenly it occurred to Jared that just possibly her husband hadn't been killed—also by strangulation—simply because some business deal with Niarchos went sour, or because Niarchos, dazzled by unexpected profit, wanted it all for himself. He couldn't pursue this line of thought to any conclusion, but in the back of his mind an uneasy suspicion was trying to form.

Sergeant Hopper, pushing aside his luncheon plate and leaning back, said, 'What are you thinking, Mr. Dexter?'

'Paul Niarchos, Sergeant; I'm thinking about him.'

Hopper smiled pleasantly. 'Well, if it'll help any, both those men he killed in Europe and bought his way clear of—were strangled to death.'

They looked at one another, Sergeant Hopper faintly smiling, unperturbed, probing, Jared surprised, baffled and emotionally concerned.

Hopper then dropped another clanger. 'By the way; your friend Mr. Steele has an interesting police record. For the past four years he's been above reproach, but were you aware that the previous three years he spent in custody for embezzlement?'

Jared had only renewed his friendship with Frederick Steele three years earlier, after an interlude of quite a number of years, since college together, but he had never enquired where Steele had been in that interim; he'd just assumed, being an accountant by trade . . .

'I'm not making any accusation,' said Hopper, in the face of Jared's expression of unpleasant surprise. 'I'm only wondering if you knew?'

'No, I didn't know, Sergeant.'

'I hardly thought so. Will it matter very much, Mr. Dexter? I mean, putting Mrs. Leeds's personal affairs in order won't give him access to any part of the Leeds fortune, will it?'

Jared said, 'No, it won't Sergeant. What were the details of Fred's conviction?'

'Well, nothing very spectacular, actually, Mr. Dexter. He was heavily in debt, perhaps through no fault of his own, I can't say. But he was comtroller for an electronics firm in Chicago.'

'Juggled the books?'

'Yes. Got off with eighty thousand dollars. Nice, round figure, eh?'

Jared was recovering slowly from the shock and simply said, 'I'll be damned. I hadn't seen Fred for years; we met by accident in a restaurant several years ago.' Jared looked sharply at Sergeant Hopper. 'You'll know, I suppose, that we went to school together?'

'I know that, yes. And just so you won't dash out there and fire him, I also know that he's been scrupulously honest since moving to New York and opening his accounting office.' Hopper glanced at his wrist. 'It's been a long morning. I really ought to be getting along, Mr. Dexter.' As Hopper rose he patted his breast to indicate the audit-report inside his coat. 'I appreciate your help very much.'

Jared laughed. 'Enough to take the tail off?'

Hopper's smile broadened. It was really a very pleasant and disarming smile, and without a shred of doubt Hopper used it exactly for those purposes. 'Of course,' he said, and left.

Jared sat a while over his coffee, then

returned to the office. The moment he walked into his reception room Miss Jorgenson informed him he'd had a call from George Alexander. He went through to the private office and drew the telephone to him across the desk.

George was not at home, a servant told Jared. He asked for Fred and got him, but all Fred knew was that George had gone off, as he'd been doing the past week or so, by himself and without telling anyone at the house what he was up to.

Jared said, 'He called me a while back.'

Fred still was no help. 'He didn't tell me anything at all, Jared.'

'All right; then *you* can tell *him* something for me when he returns. First off, I'll be out later in the afternoon. Secondly, you can tell him that David Leeds's body has been exhumed by the police, and a laboratory examination indicates that Leeds did not die of the heart attack his doctor put on the Death Certificate, he was strangled to death.'

Fred said, 'Good lord,' then he rallied quickly, almost as though ashamed of being startled. 'You got that from Hopper, of course.'

'Yes. And there is one other item, Fred. Hopper has had men following all three of us.'

'Me too, Jared.'

'I said all *three* of us, Fred. He also had a man on Elbert Carling, so if George is

108

worrying about Carling dropping from sight, he can stop being anxious. And Fred— Sergeant Hopper is a person we should never sell short. Good-bye for now. Do me a favour and be around when I arrive later on.'

Fred's reply was lively with interest. 'I wouldn't miss it for the world; see you later.'

Jared rang off and sat with his hand on the telephone gazing at the instrument sardonically. Maybe Fred wouldn't be so fascinated when they went off privately to talk!

Reginald Morgan telephoned a little later, as Jared was drawing up the rough draft of an appeal to be submitted to a Superior Court Judge on an estate he'd only agreed to represent a few weeks earlier, and it left him a little annoyed because, whether everyone with whom he'd been involved lately thought so or not, he had other obligations than just the Leeds Estate.

Old Morgan said, 'Did you get the copy of that silly audit, Jared? Because if you've passed it along to the police or someone, they may not like it.'

Jared had a bad premonition and groaned aloud. 'Why not? What's happened now, for the lord's sake!'

'Someone deposited thirty thousand dollars yesterday, by mail.'

Jared's irritation mounted. 'What do you mean—someone. People have to sign cheques, Reginald.'

'Cash, my boy, thirty thousand cash in an envelope with a deposit slip already made out.'

Jared leaned far back at the desk and let his gaze wander to the far window. Beyond it, high in the westward sky, a streak of silver was winging its way across a cloudless sky. 'Elbert Carling,' said Jared. 'The damned fool.'

Morgan agreed. 'Anyone would have to be one, you know, simply to stuff thirty thousand in cash into an envelope and mail it. Even assuming the postal people are all saints, there is never any such guarantee with bank employees even though we screen them to beat the devil before they're hired. But in any case, Jared, you'd better make a notation in that audit-report that general personal funds have been increased thirty thousand dollars' worth, or the thing is going to look pretty bad, eh?'

George put aside the telephone and turned to see if that aeroplane was still in sight. It was not, but it hadn't been any more than a symbol anyway; by now, eight or ten hours later, Elbert Carling was back on earth again, in London.

He left the office, telling Miss Jorgenson he probably wouldn't be back for the rest of the day, and drove thoughtfully out to the Leeds mansion. It was slightly past three in the afternoon when he wheeled up into the driveway and saw a spanking-new Jaguar X-series car parked out in front. He walked over to look inside. The car had that soul-satisfying fragrance of all new cars. Also, it showed on the temporary owner's certificate, that its legal owner was George Alexander. In other circumstances Jared might have smiled with a feeling of paternal indulgence. It was exactly the kind of car a single man of thirty would want.

But he didn't smile, indulgently or any other way, as he turned and walked on up to the door. He'd had too many jolts lately to be able to smile about much of anything.

Fred answered the door and shook his head even before Jared asked the question. 'Nope; he hasn't telephoned nor returned. I would be inclined to expect him shortly though. Come on into the study, I've been making some final drafts.'

Jared, following along, said, 'Are you finished, then?'

'Just about. Another day or two ought to do it.'

As they entered the dark, wood-panelled study Jared closed the door and stood back by it while Fred went back around the table where he'd been working, sat, then looked at Jared with a forming expression of enquiry.

Jared didn't mince words. 'Fred, the police have dug up your embezzlement record in Chicago.'

Steele was still and unblinking for a moment, then rocked forward with a nod of his head. 'I expected it. I should have told you, of course, and that's why you're angry.'

'I'm not angry, Fred. I'm not sure I'm even disappointed. But it shook my confidence in you. I'll admit that very frankly.'

'It happened a long time back, Jared.' Steele didn't look up now; he caught hold of a pencil and rolled it slowly between his palms. 'I didn't tell you I was married, either. Well, I was, and that was why I did it. The money was there, I needed it very badly, and I took it. Of course I was caught.' Steele finally raised his face. 'I was tried, sentenced, and if I hadn't been able to give back seventy thousand I'd have had to serve a longer term.'

'And your wife?'

Fred smiled like a death's-head. 'What do you think? She left me, of course—with what remained of the ten thousand I didn't return. I've never heard from her since.' He flung down the pencil, shot up to his feet and walked to a window. 'So now you know, and now you pull me off the Steele account—and forget you ever knew me.'

Jared almost said something emotional, but in the last moment got cautious. 'No. You finish up here. As for the other ... let's just wait and see.'

Steele turned, his mouth pulled down. 'Alexander ...?'

Jared hadn't thought of whether he'd tell George or not. 'I don't see much reason to tell him, Fred. You'll be through in a day or two.'

Fred kept watching Jared, and after a while he smiled at him. 'Sure. And I've put you in a hell of a spot. I understand.'

Jared saw the electric coffee pot and moved towards it. He didn't particularly want a cup of the stuff, but neither did he like the atmosphere of the room right then. 'Care for java?' he asked, to change the mood of the study.

Outside, a taxi drew up. They both turned towards the window in time to see George Alexander pay the driver and head for the house.

CHAPTER THIRTEEN

IDENTITY OF A MURDERER!

George walked into the study with a brisk step and a nod for the room's other occupants, who were having coffee. Without looking at either of them he said, 'I suppose you deplore my extravagance in buying the Jaguar.'

Fred didn't even bother speaking; he was simply an employee. The three of them had been somewhat closer than most employees and employers become, but Fred was still just an employee. He returned to the front window where sunshine splashed against the front of the mansion, and sipped his coffee over there. Also, he had something more private on his mind than someone's purchase of a new car.

Jared only said, 'It's a beautiful piece of machinery, George. By the way, Sergeant Hopper had David Leeds exhumed. Pathological run-down indicates he was strangled to death.'

Jared might as well have commented on the beautiful day outside; George, in the act of filling a cup at the coffee urn, neither looked around nor even paused at his work. Jared dropped another bombshell.

'Carling mailed thirty thousand cash to the bank yesterday. They got it this morning. We'll all understand why he did it.'

George finally looked up. 'Not very logical of him, though. The cat's already out of the bag between Carling and Niarchos. I mean, *we* know, and I assume that by now Hopper also knows. Niarchos may not know, but returning the thirty thousand isn't going to change anything, is it?'

'Maybe he had a conscience,' said Jared.

George shrugged, finished drawing his coffee, turned and looked at Fred Steele's back. Jared thought there was a peculiar hard expression in George's gaze but wasn't sure. Then George faced Jared.

'Would you like to know where I've been most of this day?'

Jared was annoyed by the question. 'Riddles are for children,' he said, and went to a chair to sit down.

George smiled at him. 'You haven't been getting enough sleep lately, Jared. Don't answer; I know it's all my fault. Anyway, I've been doing some digging on Paul Niarchos, your friend.'

'Not *my* friend, dammit.'

George blinked and even Fred turned at the sharpness of Jared's retort. George smiled again. 'Excuse me. Forget I said it. It was only a kind of poor joke anyway.' He shook his head. 'You *are* getting testy, Jared.'

'All right,' exclaimed Jared, controlling his irritation with an effort. 'You've got the facetiousness off your chest. Now tell us what you have been doing with Mr. Niarchos.'

'Not *with* him; he's in Europe. As a matter of fact he is in Paris.' George let that lie there for a moment because of its undeniable novelty. 'What I couldn't work out satisfactorily is whether Carling knew where Niarchos was when he fled last night. I got the impression from Carling that he was fleeing *from* Niarchos, not straight into his arms.'

Jared rose, stepped to the telephone and dialled Sergeant Hopper's number. He didn't expect to get the detective and he didn't, but he got someone who promised to locate Hopper at once and relay any message, so Jared explained about Niarchos and Carling both being in Europe. Afterwards, resuming his seat, he nodded at George. 'Go on. What else have you turned up, Mr. Holmes?'

115

'That Paul Niarchos has a rather large holding company based in Paris, but with large Middle East investments.'

Jared was unimpressed. 'George, for your information Paul Niarchos is an international financier on the large scale. If you'd looked up Richard Bellah you'd have found a very similar background, or any of the other people who—'

'With a holding company, Paris-based, whose wealth has skyrocketed the past three years, or during the international gold scares of late, because it is capitalized in pure gold ingots?'

Fred went to the desk, sat down, lit a cigarette and said, 'The dental gold again.'

George and Jared acted as though he hadn't spoken. As they looked directly at one another Jared said, 'So the partnership wasn't dissolved because that Leeds-Niarchos business combine failed to pay off.'

'It was dissolved,' said George, 'because it *was* paying off, and in such a spectacular manner that no one could have anticipated it, but evidently, I would say, sufficiently to warrant someone's death.'

Jared nodded, but all he said was: 'A neat assumption, but is there one shred of proof?'

George smiled. 'Counsellor, I'm first-off a human being, and only secondly law-orientated, but that same thought crossed my mind this morning, so I bought us a gentleman named Hershey. Mr. Hershey used to look

116

after Paul Niarchos's U.S. interests.'

Fred interrupted. 'Not *Jerome* Hershey.'

George turned slightly. 'The same. Tell us about him, Fred.'

'He's one of the most eminent accountants in the city. Why, Hershey and Stone Company have set up accounting systems for all the really large New York City businesses. George, if you bought him you didn't do it for peanuts.'

That, it turned out, was very true. 'One hundred thousand dollars,' nodded George. 'And even then I didn't get much more than I've just told you.'

'But there was *some* more,' said Fred.

'Enough, I suppose. Paul Niarchos asked Mrs. Leeds to marry him. Hershey told me Niarchos told him that. Mr. Niarchos also told him he'd heard from Paris last year that someone had been over there asking questions. He traced it back to an American, by all descriptions, named Jones. John Jones.'

Jared began wagging his head. 'Using an alias won't save Carling. Not if Paul Niarchos really wants to know who ...' He suddenly snapped his mouth closed and looked up. 'Anything else, George?'

'Some details on how the dental gold was spread around in Europe, but Mr. Hershey really didn't have very much on that. It was outside his sphere.'

Fred, watching Jared, softly said, 'Okay. What just came to you?'

117

Jared's reply was flat. 'That Niarchos *did* find out who the American was who called himself Jones.'

George went to a chair, finished his coffee and leaned to set aside the cup as he said, 'I thought of that, Jared. But Carling-Jones is still around. If Niarchos *did* find out, why didn't he cut Carling down last year?'

Jared had no answer, but he had another comment to make. 'I don't know. Carling could tell us, perhaps. I'm afraid that unless he does tell us we're never going to know. But it's beginning to stick in my mind that his flight last night might not actually have had anything to do with escaping Paul Niarchos at all. He was fleeing from the U.S. police.'

George nodded again. 'My thinking too. And to pursue it, assuming that Niarchos knew who Jones was, why he was snooping and what he'd discovered in Paris, all this might very well account for Carling's agitation last night. *He was alive only because he had convinced Niarchos he would never mention a word of what he'd learned.*' George let that sink in before saying anything else.

Jared was lost in deep thought. Fred Steele lit a fresh cigarette, leaned back in the desk-chair with both hands clasped behind his head and studied George Alexander, who eventually went on speaking.

'How Carling managed to convince Niarchos, who has to be an unprincipled man, not to kill him. I can't imagine, but he certainly must have managed it somehow.'

Jared had an explanation to that but he didn't want to offer it just yet. *Carling, not Niarchos, had killed Elizabeth Leeds!*

He said, 'And I was calling Carling all kinds of an idiot this morning for flying off to London and practically into the arms of his mortal enemy who was just across the Channel.' He rose and went across to the front window. 'Why in the hell didn't we call Sergeant Hopper last night, when Carling was still here?'

No one answered him.

Moments later a light knock on the study door brought George to his feet. It was one of the house staff asking if the gentlemen would care to have a highball before supper. George said the gentlemen would indeed like highballs, returned to his chair with the door left open, and crossed both legs at the ankles as he made a study of the far wall, which was book-lined.

'I've got to go upstairs for a moment,' he said, making no immediate move to rise. 'Jared? What do you think of someone going to Paris?'

Jared turned from the window. 'Whatever for?'

'To get Carling to come back, of course.'

'All you'll get,' said Fred Steele through a bluish cloud of fragrant smoke, 'is someone's head bashed in, or a garrotte round their neck,

119

George.'

'But we've got to have him back in the U.S. Even Hopper can't do any more with an extradition order than scare him into hiding, and then we just may lose the man altogether.'

'He wouldn't return,' surmised Jared. 'Whether he thinks we may be this far along towards nailing him, he isn't going to risk his neck when he doesn't have to.'

George rose, plunged both hands into his trouser pockets and stood gazing absently at the floor a moment. Then he brisked up. 'I'll be back in a little while.'

After he'd left the study their highballs arrived. Both Jared and Fred downed theirs and sent for refills. Fred was his normal sanguine self by this time. He said he thought they shouldn't even consider George's scheme, but should leave the extradition of Elbert Carling to Sergeant Hopper.

Jared was in agreement, but without any enthusiasm, because he was convinced, with no motivation at all, and with appreciable risk if he *did* return, Carling was not going to be easy to apprehend. He re-stated his earlier comment and Fred shrugged, smoked a while staring at the opened door, and after an interval of some moments, said, 'We're not going to do any more than tread water without him, Jared. Maybe it wouldn't be too far off if one of us *did* try George's method.'

Jared's exasperation rang out when he

replied. 'How? By twisting Carling's arm all the way up the airport-ramp? Don't be ridiculous, Fred. Hopper will either have to come up with something, or we'll just have to take our chances.'

Fred gave that sardonic smile of his. 'How good are they, Jared?'

'Admittedly not very good. But I'm not going to stand by while you or George try kidnapping Carling. Even if we had *evidence*, which we don't have, we'd be in almost as much hot water for abducting Carling as he'd be if we could prove he was a murderer.'

Fred hauled straight up in his chair. 'A— murderer?'

Jared hadn't meant to say it. It was what he'd thought a short while back, but he hadn't wished to say it just yet. Now though, his slip had destroyed the secret, so he said, 'Look, Fred; I can think of only one really sound reason why Paul Niarchos didn't go after Carling, when he found out who Jones was.'

'Carling—murdered Elizabeth Leeds?'

'It's just a wild guess. But if Niarchos let Carling live, there had to be the best of all reasons. The best one *I* can come up with is that Paul Niarchos didn't kill Elizabeth, Carling did. Perhaps under orders from Niarchos— who knows?'

'Are you going to tell this to George?'

'I suppose so. Why not?'

'Because,' said Fred. 'he's already balancing

on the brink of flying to London or Paris, that's why not. I've lived here in the house with him for some time, Jared. I think I know how he reacts about as well as you do. Give him that much scent of the killer, and he'll fly out of here tonight. Tomorrow he'll either get himself killed, or he'll be embroiled in that abduction-business you just spoke of.'

It made sense. Jared turned as their fresh drinks came, took his, waited until the servant had soundlessly departed, then hoisted the glass in mock-salute. 'To our secret. I won't tell him, then.'

The telephone rang. It was Sergeant Hopper. He had thought Jared might be at the Leeds place, and he wanted to thank him for the relayed information concerning Niarchos being in Europe also.

Jared said, 'Meet me at my office after dinner this evening. There is a little more to discuss.' He slammed down the telephone as Hopper started to say something, because he heard George coming down the stairs two at a time.

Fred stubbed out his cigarette and rose, looking a little less ironically self-assured than he usually looked.

CHAPTER FOURTEEN

A NEAR THING

When Jared met Sergeant Hopper that evening at his office the building rang hollowly each time a maintenance man walked down a corridor and although the automatic lighting made the interior of the place as bright as day, it had a tomb-like atmosphere throughout.

Hopper looked rumpled, like a man who has been long in his clothing, but he neither acted tired nor complained of having to meet Jared so long after the close of the normal working day. He did, however, say that one of the advantages of being a subordinate policeman was the ability to watch most of the worthwhile television shows.

Jared explained about his earlier meeting with Fred Steele and George Alexander. He told Hopper every bit of what the three of them had evolved by way of possibilities was without substantiation. He even told Hopper of his personal theory about Carling being the killer of Elizabeth Leeds.

The sergeant was agreeable with everything up to that point, and while he did not scoff, he made several rather pointedly sceptical remarks.

'You've come up with an interesting

hypothesis,' he told Jared, 'but you've done it about like the man who climbed stairs backwards so he could see where he'd been rather than where he was going. In other words, while you like the idea of Carling fleeing the local police, you haven't yet given me one *reason* for him to have killed Mrs. Leeds.'

Jared obliged. 'Go back a bit to the time Carling went snooping over in Paris. He tried to cover his tracks. Not very well, I admit. Carling after all was better at exposing than anything else. Still, he did his best, and even though it required a little time for Niarchos to hear someone had been snooping around, and more time for him to cut through Carling's little subterfuges of identity, Niarchos eventually did it, Sergeant.'

'So ...?'

'So when he finally cornered Elbert Carling the price of survival for Carling was the death of Elizabeth Leeds. Niarchos wins both ways—which is his customary way of doing business. He silenced Carling for ever, and he got Elizabeth killed without having any personal involvement at all. You could even say, he'd taught Carling a lesson: If you play games in Niarchos's league, you'd better be prepared to give more than just your life if you lose—your soul as well.'

'It's nice,' said Hopper. 'Very neat and reasonable, Mr. Dexter.'

Jared waved a hand. 'Don't say it, Sergeant.

It's nice, but there isn't a shred of truth.'

'Right you are, Mr. Dexter.' Hopper smiled. 'Or am I wrong?'

'You are quite right. But don't we have to work from some kind of hypothesis? How many crimes are solved because the police have courtroom-proof every inch of the way?'

Hopper chuckled. 'None, I'm afraid. To get back to Mrs. Leeds; you say she was killed because she discovered Niarchos had her husband killed. Is that right?'

'It may be, Sergeant, but I rather doubt it. Her husband died half a decade ago. In that length of time it seems improbable to me, having known her, that she wouldn't have gone to the police. I'd say she didn't know her husband had been strangled, accepted the doctor's verdict of a heart attack—but *last* year she somehow discovered just how much Niarchos had euchred her husband out of.'

'And went to him to make the accusation?'

Jared squirmed. 'Perhaps, but I just can't see Elizabeth Leeds being that foolhardy.'

Hopper threw up his hands. 'Then there is only one alternative left—*he* discovered how much she had found out, and made the deal with Carling. If he'd kill her, Niarchos would let Carling live.'

Jared nodded and Sergeant Hopper leaned back in his chair to study the ceiling briefly before he said, 'Well, in some ways it fits with the investigation Harlow and I have been making into the backgrounds of all these people—you included, Mr. Dexter.' Hopper dropped his eyes, smiled and said, 'We had to discard you pretty early in the investigation though. You were never in the right place at the right time. But then we had to drop Richard Bellah, our other prime suspect too. He was playing in a country club tennis tournament the day Mrs. Leeds was killed, and we were able to ascertain that at the time of her husband's murder some years back, he was on a yacht race to the Bahamas. Still, I never actually thought any of you people, considering your wealth, would actually do those little jobs yourself. Niarchos was the sole exception. He personally strangled those men in Europe.' Hopper yawned behind one big paw. 'Mr. Dexter, it's never been a real hard case right from the start, except in one way: I was dealing with some very influential people. I couldn't run around making myself obnoxious without there being some nasty repercussions through the Police Commissioner. So, what I've always needed is what I *still* need; some kind of proof. Something strong enough so that if I arrest Niarchos, Carling, or someone else, it won't all blow up in my face and get the city sued.' Hopper leaned in his chair. 'Now that you've also come to this realization— produce some proof, Mr. Dexter. We've got all the theory we need. Give me some kind of evidence that will permit me to order an arrest

126

or two, because frankly, I'm stymied. I can't move one more step until I can come up with some damned good proof against a murderer. We both know murder has been committed, but that by itself doesn't do much more than make it a police affair. Do you see my point?'

Jared saw it. He also saw something else: Hopper's stalemate. He asked about the scene of Elizabeth's murder and Hopper gave him a woeful look.

'If there'd been anything there, Mr. Dexter, you can bet good money that by now we'd have made an arrest. There was nothing; no fingerprints, no witnesses, not even anyone who heard the struggle. He caught her from behind at her dressing-table. Even the suggestion Harlow made to me that she knew him or he'd never have been able to come up like that when she could see behind her in the mirror, doesn't hold water. He could have come in from either side and had her on her back before she could even scream. Any of the bruises on her face and head could have come from a blow that stunned her. Hell, Mr. Dexter, we're not even sure which method he used in entering the house. When I got out there half the downstairs doors were unlocked, and even more of the windows, although closed, had not been latched.'

Jared nodded sympathetically. 'So you went for suspects.'

'We had to, Mr. Dexter. We didn't have

another damned thing.'

'Including me.'

'You know how that is. We take all her friends first, then her acquaintances, and we start going through backgrounds, finances, affairs of the heart, and try to put together a nice bunch to work from.'

'Okay, Sergeant, that's where we are now.'

'Except for one thing: no proof, Mr. Dexter. You give me anything worthwhile at all and I'll jump in with both feet.'

Jared glanced at his wrist. It was nine o'clock, which surprised him. They'd been talking for hours. Hopper, seeing that motion with the wristwatch, sighed and picked his battered hat off the corner of the desk, then rose. 'I've enjoyed talkin' to you. I think you're probably right all the way down the line.'

Jared smiled. 'But—no proof.' He rose to see Sergeant Hopper out. 'All right; give me a day or so to work on that at my end while you're doing some digging on your end. Between the two of us...'

The telephone rang, startling both men. Jared picked it up and Fred Steele's voice came down the line in staccato sentences.

'George drove off in the Jaguar about fifteen minutes ago, Jared. He didn't say a word to me, not even when I asked what he was up to. Also, he had a bag packed.'

Jared made a blasphemous remark, then thanked Fred, dropped the telephone and turned towards Hopper. 'Use your authority, Sergeant.' He held the telephone towards Hopper. 'George Alexander is heading for the airport right this minute to take an overnight flight to Europe for the purpose of kidnapping Carling and bringing him back.'

Hopper may have been surprised but he didn't show it. Instead he took the telephone, stepped closer and dialled swiftly. He fired sentences at whoever answered at the other end.

'The name is George Alexander. Description: an inch or two over six feet, about thirty years of age, dark hair, blue eyes, bronze colouring, handsome, driving Jaguar car. He'll try to book flight to either Paris or London out of Kennedy International Airport. Stop him … Use any charge that comes to mind. No, don't make an arrest, just an apprehension. Bring him to the booking office. I'll be down there waiting.'

Hopper replaced the telephone gently and turned, frowning. 'He's a hot-head, Mr. Dexter. That kind of a person can get into a lot of trouble.'

Although Jared was inclined to agree, there was another side to it, which he mentioned. 'He's been waiting around for a month, Sergeant, for the police to come up with something.'

Hopper wasn't impressed. 'Mr. Dexter, in case you didn't know it, the police very rarely solve serious crimes short of six months, regardless of what they write in the magazines.' Hopper resumed his way towards the outer office and the yonder doorway out into the corridor. 'One other thing; this damned fool is going to be the cause of me losing a night's sleep, and I don't take kindly to that either.'

'What will you do with him?'

Hopper turned, dumping the hat on the back of his head. 'Start by reading the riot act to him. After that it's up to him.'

'Call me at home,' said Jared, and closed the door gently as Sergeant Hopper went marching down the empty corridor.

He went back to his private office and dialled the Leeds residence, hoping to get Fred instead of rousing one of the servants. He not only was successful, but Fred must have been sitting beside the telephone because he answered after only one ring.

'Jared Dexter here,' he said. 'Hopper has put out a hold for George at the airport. They'll get him, I'm confident of that, but what has he said to you since I was there last?'

'That's just it,' replied Steele. 'Nothing. He's gone around with his hands in his pockets looking like a time-bomb waiting to explode. I tried to talk to him and it was like making conversation with a stone wall. Then, just a little while ago, he went off to his room, and I was finishing up here in the study when he went dashing by with a suitcase in hand. I called but he didn't even look round. Then I heard the car start and ran out, but he was already half-way to the street, so I came back and buzzed you . . . Jared, what did Hopper have to say?'

'Just exactly what we might have expected, Fred. Without some kind of proof, we've got a great big armload of air.'

Jared rang off, went about closing his offices for the night, and with the lonely sound of his footfalls for companionship, departed from the building. Outside, there was less traffic, of course, than there would have been had it been broad daylight, but there was still enough to require all his skill for the drive to the hotel where he lived.

There, too, although a few night-owls were in the lobby, reading newspapers, chatting, moving in that somewhat aimless way of insomniacs, the place was relatively quiet.

He took the lift to his rooms, thought about mixing himself a highball before retiring, decided not to, showered, then went to bed.

And lay for another hour and a half until even the night-owl sounds of the city diminished to a quiet, distant kind of daytime echo, trying to marshal a lot of complicated facets into an understandable composite, and in the middle of it all he finally fell asleep.

The bedside telephone brought him wide awake with a pounding heart after only a short while of sleep. It was Sergeant Hopper sounding both tired and sardonic.

'We got him all right, and you were right, the damned fool had just bought a ticket to London. Fortunately though, his flight wouldn't have pulled out until five this morning.'

'What was his reaction?'

Hopper seemed to hesitate a little before answering. 'Well, Mr. Dexter, let me put it this way; if I hadn't been a cop, and if I'd been fifteen years younger, I'd have knocked out half his teeth for him.'

'I'm sorry, Sergeant.'

Hopper said, 'Don't be. It's part of my job. But then you'll be coming in for your share tomorrow, because he thinks you and Mr. Steele turned him in to us. Anyway, I got one hard-wrung promise out of him: He wouldn't try this again for at least a week, providing we come up with something before then. So—get me some proof will you, please? Good night, Mr. Dexter.'

Jared put aside the telephone, sat a moment on the edge of the bed, then almost laughed. It was getting so complicated, so difficult, so tangled and unpredictable that just simply going to bed was no longer any guarantee that a person could even sleep.

CHAPTER FIFTEEN

RETURN OF THE PRODIGAL

Jared had court the following morning, early. After that, and even though he got out an hour earlier than he'd expected, there were three wealthy clients waiting when he got back to the office.

By noon he'd managed to transact as much business as he wished to, and that left him feeling satisfied. For several weeks now he'd been putting things off because of the Leeds affair.

Lovely Miss Jorgenson eyed him with misgiving as he emerged from the private office shortly after two in the afternoon. 'If you're leaving,' she said, 'would you please leave a number where you can be reached, Mr. Dexter, because there was a call a while ago...'

He gave her the unlisted Leeds telephone number and left the office, went down to his car and drove to Hyde Park through a day so sparkling and sweet-scented that it had to belong somewhere else, not around New York City.

Fred Steele met him after a servant had answered his ring. Fred smiled, led the way to the study, stepped to the desk and held up a somewhat voluminous series of pages encased in a canary-yellow, deckled folder. He dropped the manuscript-sized book.

'The end. Madame's personal accounts brought current, her bills paid, and beyond all that, in the back I've appended a chart plus instructions for anyone who takes over this end of the estate. Guidelines, they are commonly called.' Fred grinned. 'Now join George and his father at the poolside, if you wish. Personally, I've left them alone this morning.'

'Anything wrong?' asked Jared, and Fred gave him a rather questioning look.

'*Everything* is wrong, as if you didn't know it. But no, everything else aside, there's nothing wrong. It's just that his father seems to me to be failing pretty fast now. I figured they'd want to be left alone. Coffee?'

'No, thanks,' said Jared, and strolled out of the study, on through to the glass-walled conservatory where there was an excellent view of the entire rear grounds, and saw father and son out in the warm and wonderful sunlight at the pool's edge.

He'd thought of several things to tell George, about that foolish escapade of the night before, but they didn't seem to fit the mood at the poolside so he returned to the study, content to abide by Fred Steele's suggestion, oblique though it was, to leave father and son alone.

Fred was smoking when Jared returned. He looked up from behind the desk where he was sitting and asked a question with his eyes, to which Jared replied that there wasn't anything, he supposed that couldn't wait a bit.

Fred nodded. 'There was a doctor here this morning. I didn't speak with him but George did, and if his face was any indication afterwards, I'd say his father is in pretty bad shape.'

Jared had never doubted it. Spiegelman had said a month to a month and a half. That had been a week and more ago. Jared told Fred about his talk with Sergeant Hopper as a matter of course. They were interrupted once, when the telephone rang and it was Jared's secretary saying a gentleman had called for an appointment but had declined to give his name. That wasn't as unusual as it sounded; Jared was not the only high-priced lawyer who got those calls from free-advice seekers. He asked his girl if there was anything else. She said there was; that a client had called to ask Jared if he would be available the following week, when the client returned from holiday, to make changes in the client's will. Miss Jorgenson chuckled. 'Evidently the holiday wasn't as blissful as he thought it ought to have been. Otherwise, Mr. Morgan called from the bank and wants you to call back at your convenience.'

Jared thanked his secretary, replaced the telephone and sought for the topic he was discussing with Fred when they'd been interrupted. Fred said, 'What you and Hopper came up with,' as a prompting comment.

Jared took it from there. 'It evolves around proof,' he said. 'We don't have any.'

Fred blew smoke and looked sardonic. 'Tell me something I'm not fully aware of.' He leaned back in the desk-chair. 'What about the police, and the scene of the murder? Isn't that where they usually get clues?'

'Hopper says there was nothing at all.'

'Splendid,' murmured Steele, and leaned to crush his cigarette in an ashtray. 'Maybe George would at least have stirred up something in Europe.'

'No doubt of it. *He'd* have got arrested. What we need is something that could *help*, not hinder.'

Fred's gaze fell upon the canary-yellow folder and he sighed softly. 'It's not my headache,' he said. 'I'm finished here. I'll go back to my office tomorrow.' He and Jared looked at one another. Fred's eyes crinkled faintly, in an ironic way. 'It's been interesting out here. Lucrative of course, and I'm obliged to you for that, Jared, but more than anything else it's been interesting. How many dull career pencil-pushers ever get a sideline seat at a murder?'

A shadow fell across the doorway and George appeared. He didn't smile and neither of the other men did either. He hung there, slouching in the opening, gazing at Jared.

136

'Okay, say it,' he exclaimed. 'Hopper was mad last night, and you are mad this morning. Well, I'm not altogether—'

'Forget it,' snapped Jared. 'It was stupid and I think an hour after you'd bought the ticket to London you knew it was stupid too.'

'I wanted action.'

'What the hell *kind* of action, George? Rushing off half-cocked to do something that would plaster your face in half the newspapers of the world would get the action, no doubt of that. But what *kind* of action?'

George heaved upright, ambled on into the room, dropped into a chair and said, 'Like you said, Jared. Forget it.'

'I've one question first. Are you going to keep your word to Hopper about not trying it again?'

George nodded, acting a little embarrassed as he picked a grass stem from the poolside lawn off his trouser-leg. 'I always keep my word,' he muttered, then, as though anxious to change the subject, which he doubtless was, he looked up again. 'Anything new?'

Jared shook his head. 'We need some kind of proof that Carling and Niarchos are involved in murder.'

'How about that information I bought from old Jerome Hershey about the gold business?'

'All it suggests—and doesn't prove at all—is that Leeds and Niarchos were partners years ago, then they ceased being partners. You didn't get enough from Hershey even to prove Paul Niàrchos had beaten either David or Elizabeth Leeds out of a penny. But even if you could prove that, it's not much to base a murder complaint upon.'

George said, 'Dead-end, Jared?'

It seemed that way, no doubt of it. Jared decided sitting here with his friends wasn't going to help any either, so he rose, saying he'd return to the office and try to think of something.

Neither of them tried to dissuade him. In fact, as the three of them parted, it seemed that there was not an additional original thought among them. Which there wasn't.

On the drive back to the heart of the city Jared racked his brain for something that would get the investigation moving again. It had ground to a halt because of lack of evidence, and somehow he had to find something, or perhaps manufacture something, to get it going again.

Back at the office Miss Jorgenson said Mr. Morgan had called again, so Jared put in a call to the bank.

Morgan wanted to know when he could see George Alexander regarding a merger of stock-shares one of the bank's economists had decided would keep the Leeds Estate from having to pay such enormous capital-gains taxes, without actually diminishing actual dividend-revenue very much.

It sounded so boring that Jared said, 'Reginald, why don't you just call out there and ask him to drop around? This business of using me as your intermediary can't go on indefinitely in any case. As far as I'm concerned, I'd like to sign off as executor.'

'Jared, you can't do that.'

'The hell I can't. Give me one good reason, George is legal heir; it's only a question of time before the will is probated, then he'll have complete control.'

'You need a vacation. You can't be serious about throwing up the biggest account you have. Moreover, I'm not at all satisfied with that damned quickie audit the bank made.'

'I didn't say I'd throw up the Leeds Estate, Reginald. I'll still handle it in the legal capacity—if George wishes me to ... What did you say about that audit?'

'It isn't specific enough. It was done in too much of a hurry.'

'Perhaps, what you need, is to have an outside auditor spend a few months doing a thorough and professional job.'

'I realize that.'

'I'll send a man around in the morning.'

'Hmmmm! Is this some private axe you have to grind, Jared?'

'You could say that, Reginald. Only this man also happens to be one of the best in the business.'

'Well ... I had in mind talking to Jerome

Hershey.'

'He is old, Reginald, semi-retired, and acts mostly in an advisory capacity now. What you need is someone who can jump in with both feet and work the—'

'I know what I need, damn it all, Jared!'

'Good. Then I'll send him over in the morning. You make a point of being there to see him personally.'

'All right. All right. Before you hang up tell me—is there anything new on Elizabeth's murder?'

'There is quite a bit new, yes, but it's not putting the police very much closer to an arrest.'

'How can that be?'

Jared sighed. 'You'll read all about it in the newspapers one of these days. Good-bye, Reginald.'

He put aside the telephone, scratched the tip of his nose and swivelled the chair to reach for one of several manila folders Miss Jorgenson had neatly and discreetly placed on the right side of his large desk, each folder having a little typed notation as to why he should familiarize himself with the contents before seeing some client or other.

The telephone jangled at his elbow. He glared at it, willing to react with hostility except that the confounded apparatus wouldn't cease its shrill periodic ringing. He snatched it up and Miss Jorgenson's throaty voice said, 'Mr. Dexter? There is a gentleman in the outer office to see you.'

'Who?' he growled.

'Mr. Paul Niarchos.'

Jared didn't believe it. 'Who did you say he was, Eloise?'

'Mr. Paul Niarchos, sir.'

Jared started to rise before he'd even told her to send Mr. Niarchos in. He was waiting with a pounding heart when the door opened, Niarchos entered and Miss Jorgenson afterwards closed the door.

Niarchos, an almost swarthy, dark-complexioned man, had the springy step of an athlete, and he looked fit enough to be one despite the grey above the ears and the lines to his square-jawed face. He smiled and extended a hand as he approached the desk.

'It's been quite a while,' he told Jared. 'Since before Liz Leeds died, in fact, Jared.' The smile was genuine, the handclasp strong. Jared offered his visitor a chair. As Niarchos seated himself he said, 'Just flew in from Europe a couple of hours ago, Jared. Thought I'd stop by and see how you were doing.'

If Niarchos had come directly to Jared's office, he'd have a very good reason. In fact, Paul Niarchos, the international entrepreneur, never did anything without a very good reason. It crossed Jared's mind that Niarchos had seen Carling in Europe; had been informed by Carling what George, Fred Steele and he had

141

wrung out of Carling in the way of information. It wasn't a very pleasant thing to reflect upon. Niarchos's presence, like his smile, could be very menacing.

Jared sat down, leaned upon the desk and said, 'You're looking very well, Paul.'

'Been lying round the beaches,' grinned Niarchos, his black eyes soft and friendly-seeming. 'Maybe that's what you need, Jared—a month or two of loafing. Let me remind you that there are no pockets in a shroud. Spend it while you are here. Right?'

Jared kept smiling, but it struck him as extraordinary that Niarchos had mentioned a shroud and a long vacation in their first verbal exchange.

CHAPTER SIXTEEN

JARED'S SCHEME

Miss Jorgenson buzzed Jared to ask if he needed her for the rest of the day, because if he did not she would like to leave now in order to do some shopping.

'Go ahead,' he told her. 'One thing you can do first, Eloise. Give Fred Steele a ring and ask him to see me here in the office first thing in the morning.'

Miss Jorgenson said, 'Yes, sir. And thank

you.'

As Jared put aside the telephone Paul Niarchos smiled as though he understood how it was between employer and employee. But it also struck Jared that Niarchos was waiting for him to get their conversation going, and he couldn't for the life of him think of anything to say beyond a few banalities.

'Spring has finally arrived,' he said, and almost groaned aloud it sounded so utterly infantile.

But Niarchos, still smiling, went along with it. 'Beautiful weather the past week or so. I was on the Costa Brava, then over to Athens, and finally, back to the Riviera. It was wonderful.'

Jared was sure that it had been wonderful. He'd never been to any of those places, and furthermore he'd never had any desire to visit them.

Niarchos said, 'I saw a few people we both know, and of course they were saddened by Elizabeth's passing.' He mentioned several names, and although Jared knew who the people were because he'd been at the Hyde Park mansion when they had also been there, it was purest flattery for Niarchos to say Jared *knew* those people.

'Things won't be quite the same,' murmured Niarchos, his smile turning obediently melancholy. 'For me especially, it won't be the same again.' He didn't bother to explain, not that it would have been necessary in any event, but perhaps the best emphasis was in the fact that he did *not* do it. He was, in silence, admitting his love for Elizabeth Leeds.

Jared was slightly more practical. He said, 'Not for anyone else who was connected with her, Paul.'

Niarchos nodded his head in an aggrieved manner, his dark eyes lifting, eventually, and lingering upon Jared's face. 'Do the police know who killed her, Jared? Surely it has been long enough for them to find out, hasn't it?'

'They haven't confided in me,' Jared replied, treading uncertain ground with great caution. 'They come round and ask questions. They also go out to Hyde Park.'

'Tell me about her son,' said Niarchos. 'Is he like her?'

Jared could reply to this without hesitation. 'Hardly like her at all,' he said. 'He has her eyes, but they are different. Otherwise, he resembles his father—who is living there with him, incidentally. The father is dying of a brain tumour.'

'Inoperable?'

'Yes.'

'Too bad, Jared. About this son. Does eighty million dollars stagger him? I mean, will he be the passive type who will settle down to the good life and let other things slide past?'

Jared thought he understood the significance behind that question, but of course couldn't be sure. Not with Paul Niarchos, he couldn't be sure. His answer was therefore non-committal. 'He's athletic, Paul. He bought a Jaguar car, his first indication of extravagance. Otherwise, he is inclined to stay pretty close to the house—to his father. I would hazard the guess—'

Niarchos interrupted. 'But he didn't know Elizabeth. As I understood it from something I read in a newspaper, she put him in expensive private schools and did not go to see him, nor have him brought to New York. How could he feel much about her passing, I wonder?'

Jared, still straddling the fence, said, 'It might answer your question, Paul, if I told you that he never refers to her any way but as Mrs. Leeds.'

Niarchos seemed to have the answer he was seeking, because that wide smile broke over his face again. Then he switched the subject.

A little later Niarchos lighted a Turkish cigarette that had the unique distinction of smelling like a richly-endowed compost pile.

Otherwise the visit, although keeping Jared on pins-and-needles, went rather amicably and well. Paul was amusing at times, perhaps allegorical at other times although Jared was never quite sure, and before he knew it, there was a sootiness to the daylight and Niarchos sprang up apologizing for having wasted so much of Jared's time—and finally came to what he termed the purpose of his visit.

'Jared, I need your professional services.'

Dexter laughed and spread his arms wide. 'I'm an estate attorney, Paul, not an industrial nor commercial one.'

'But that's exactly why I need you. I haven't made much attempt at organizing my wealth. I would like you to advise me from time to time. For example, you know ways to consolidate stocks, to exploit tax loopholes, and I need that kind of aid.' Niarchos reached inside his coat. 'I made out this cheque for you on the flight home. You know how it is. A man is always in a hurry.' He dropped the cheque on Jared's desk. It was for the amount of two hundred and fifty thousand dollars. Jared looked up. A quarter of a million! 'That's far too much in any case,' he said, and would have added more—that he hadn't the time to take any new clients—but Niarchos waved his hand.

'Amortize it, Jared. Whatever the regular fee is, consider this the adequate retainer for as long as it entitles me to your services. Afterwards, remind me and I'll see that you are paid in advance again.' Niarchos went to the door and reached for the knob. 'As soon as I've got things at my New York office straightened out, I'll drop by again. You can start earning your fee, eh? It's been very nice seeing you again ... And I almost forgot—I ran across Bert Carling in Paris. He said to convey to you his regards when I got back.'

Niarchos left. Jared stood behind the desk gazing at the cheque for a quarter of a million dollars, and had no illusions at all about what would be expected of him as Paul Niarchos's man from now on—absolute, blind loyalty.

He put the cheque in his desk, locked the drawer and departed from the office, hungry, tired—and very puzzled.

After dinner at the dining-room of his hotel he went up to his suite, turned on some music, and made himself a stiff martini which he took to a tall window overlooking the city, and thoughtfully sipped.

One thing was certain: Paul Niarchos was an enigma, and a very experienced one at that. If Jared chose to interpret the man's visit to his office as some kind of warning, it was very easy to pick out each salient factor. If, on the other hand, Niarchos was actually offering to buy Jared's silence and services, he had just as competently got that across.

The problem, of course, was to guess which it was, and if he guessed wrong ... Niarchos had a record for deadliness that made it seem he did not spend any time listening to excuses nor apologies.

Jared was inclined to think the visit was both a warning and an offer of paid friendship— amply paid friendship at that. Otherwise, why, at the very last moment, had Niarchos mentioned seeing Carling in Paris.

Carling in Paris—Niarchos in New York! Jared stiffened as the idea came to him. It was almost too simple. He downed his drink, stepped to the telephone and began an expensive and tedious search for the hotel Elbert Carling was staying at in London.

When he ultimately got that name and number, he put in a transatlantic telephone call to the hotel, not to Carling, and something like sixty-dollars-worth later, he had the Paris address he'd started out to find.

He then sat down and wrote several drafts to a cablegram, got one that satisfied him, then wired it. When all that had been completed he made himself another, even stronger, martini, and returned to the window, beyond which his city ran as far as the horizon in all directions.

Eventually, when he retired, positive he'd lie and twist as he'd done the night before, his head barely touched the pillow before he was asleep.

The following morning he awakened needlessly early, got up, showered, shaved and dressed, then went down to his car and drove through gloomy, half-empty streets to the Leeds mansion.

There was a light on the second floor and several more lights on the groundfloor. The moment a servant answered the door, Jared caught the tantalizing aroma of coffee, eggs and bacon.

He was taken to the formal living-room while the servant, showing absolutely no surprise at his early arrival, went to inform his master that Mr. Jared Dexter was downstairs.

Ten minutes later George walked in looking shiny and fresh and fit. He threw a greeting forward, then cocked his head in a sardonic way that was slightly reminiscent of Fred Steele.

'Who built a fire under your bed this morning?' he asked. 'Had breakfast?'

'No.'

'Good. Come along, Jared.'

They went to the dining-room where a second place was swiftly set, and the food arrived at once, as though George had made this change in the previous, almost languid and indifferent way meals were served.

'Paul Niarchos came to see me yesterday,' Jared said, expecting the look of surprise George Alexander showed. 'He left a cheque for a quarter of a million dollars as a retainer, and just before leaving he said he'd seen Carling in Paris.'

George, fork in hand, gently put aside the utensil. 'Why is he back? Was the retainer a bribe?'

Jared said he had no specific answers, only some groundless guesses. He also said that after he'd thought it over, he'd come to the conclusion that if Niarchos were warning him, then there was one fairly certain way to make sure; he had sent a cablegram to Carling at his Paris address asking if Carling knew of any investigators arriving there asking questions about Paul Niarchos, after Niarchos's departure. He told George he'd signed that

149

cablegram with Niarchos's name.

George was baffled. 'What kind of sense does that make?'

'If Carling answers, he is alive. If he is alive, I'd be willing to gamble that quarter of a million dollars that whatever his intentions, when he finally sat down face to face with Niarchos, his courage evaporated and he did *not* tell Niarchos that we'd wrung some information from him. I base this on your conclusion that Carling is afraid of physical violence.'

George thought that over and eventually nodded, but not with any great show of conviction. Then he said, 'Carling will answer the cablegram, if he's alive, by addressing it to Niarchos's office. What's Niarchos going to think when he reads the answer to a cablegram he didn't send?'

'That's Sergeant Hopper's baby,' said Jared. 'And if you'll let me use the telephone in the study right now, I think I'll let Hopper try his hand at interfering with the mail.'

Jared rose, leaned upon his chair for a moment, and when George, still not eating, kept staring at the yonder wall, lost in thought, Jared turned on his heel and left the room.

Reaching Hopper proved easy. The sergeant was having coffee in his office, he confided jovially, and implored Jared not to spread the word among the other taxpayers.

Jared explained what he'd done and how

he'd done it. Hopper seemed more interested to learn Niarchos was back in the city than he was in being informed he'd have to intercept a cablegram. In fact, although Jared had expected loud protests over this, Hopper simply said he'd take care of it.

Then he said, 'It might have been better if you'd let me know in advance,' and as that mild reproof soaked in, he also said, 'Just in case you've cooked up something else, would it be asking too much to request that I be informed, now?'

'If Carling answers,' replied Jared, ignoring the sounds of reproach in Hopper's voice, 'we'll know he's alive, and we can probably also assume he lost his guts at the last moment and Niarchos still doesn't know Carling has informed against him.'

'I follow all that,' said Hopper. 'Go on. I'm sure you didn't just stop there, Mr. Dexter.' The irony was inescapable, but Jared ignored it this second time also.

'When you tell me Carling sent a cablegram, then I'll send another one, this time signing it Niarchos and telling Carling to hasten to New York, that Niarchos wants to see him immediately.'

'All that will do,' exclaimed Hopper, 'is scare him off. He'll figure Niarchos has discovered what he's done here in New York.'

'No. The cablegram will say Niarchos is about to gain control of the Leeds estate and wants Carling there to advise and suggest, on the basis of Carling's lengthy familiarity with it.'

Hopper hummed a moment then said, 'Well, it might work. I'll have to ring off now if I'm to intercept this cablegram before it's delivered. Where will you be in an hour or so?'

Jared gave two locations: the Leeds mansion or his office, put down the telephone and strolled back to finish his breakfast.

CHAPTER SEVENTEEN

AN UNEXPECTED WINDFALL

There was a rather lengthy discussion between George Alexander and Jared over the plan to trap Elbert Carling into returning to the States. George was hopeful while at the same time he was sceptical. Jared could only shrug.

'You wanted action,' he told the younger man. 'You even said I should provide it.'

George smiled, on the verge of speaking, when the nearest telephone jangled and moments later a servant came to say Mr. Dexter's office was calling.

Until Jared heard Eloise Jorgenson's voice he'd forgotten about Fred Steele. She told him Fred was there, waiting, and wondered when he'd return. Jared looked at his wrist before answering. 'Half an hour. And tell Mr. Steele

152

he is to wait.'

He returned to the dining-room to thank George for the breakfast, then departed, and by then it was well past nine o'clock in the morning, with the tag-end of tardy commuters streaming into the heart of the city. It was always this particular kind of traffic Jared sought to avoid.

He was philosophical now, as, bumper-to-bumper, he snail-paced his way towards his office building. Inevitably, he reasoned, as long as there was always this kind of traffic, regardless of how careful one was, there would be these unavoidable meetings.

He was in no big hurry in any event. Until Sergeant Hopper called to inform him that Carling had answered the cablegram, the most exciting thing on his agenda was take Fred over to meet Reginald Morgan.

There was one other thing, but until he walked into the office and saw the look on Eloise Jorgenson's face, he did not know that there was.

Fred Steele, back to the room, with a cigarette, over at a window, turned as Jared entered, nodded with that little ironic, enquiring smile, and said, 'Good morning, barrister. You keep banker's hours.'

Jared did not bother to explain that he'd been up and stirring since before sunrise. He simply said, 'Good morning,' and strode over to Miss Jorgenson's desk. She placed a typewritten note face-up so he could read it. Paul Niarchos had called; he wanted Jared to drop by his office later in the day. After lunch, specifically. He had given this information to Miss Jorgenson and had volunteered nothing more.

Jared slipped the note into his coat pocket and jerked his head for Fred to follow him into the private office. As they were taking seats Steele said, 'She's something special, isn't she? I'd forgotten.'

Jared smiled. 'She can't have been *too* special, or how could you forget?'

Steele fished for his inevitable cigarette and lit up. 'What's the mystery?' he asked.

'No mystery. The Carleton Manhattan International Bank needs an accountant who can go through the Leeds Estate from stem to stern and make an accurate, detailed breakdown.'

Steele's gaze was stone-steady as he studied Jared. 'They called you on it?'

'Yesterday. Old Reginald Morgan himself. He was talking in terms of Jerome Hershey. I only mention that so you'll have some idea of how to gauge your fee.'

'You recommended me?'

Jared brushed that aside briskly. 'You are more familiar with the personal aspects than anyone else, and from that you shouldn't have much trouble adjusting to the other aspects. Yes, I recommended you. And I'm to take you over and introduce you to old Morgan this morning. Suppose we go over there right now?' Jared wasn't altogether faking the briskness. By his private estimate he wouldn't get through at the bank until well past noon, it being almost that late now, and if he meant to keep his appointment with Niarchos he'd have to move right along.

He was half-way to the door when Fred rose and said, 'Wait a minute. You're sticking your neck out a mile, Jared. You know what I mean.'

Jared turned at the door. 'All I'm concerned with, Fred, is that you're exactly what the bank needs. As for that other matter—I don't think I'm sticking my neck out a yard, let alone a mile. Do you?'

It was a demand for candour. Steele reacted to it as though he understood perfectly. 'No,' he said quietly. 'But I want you to know—'

'Cut that out,' growled Jared. 'It's embarrassing. Come along, I'm running on a tight schedule today.'

They didn't mention Fred Steele's unhappy Chicago interlude again. Not then, and not later when there was time for reflection for both of them.

Old Morgan was waiting and his nature being as it was, he couldn't help getting off one disagreeable comment. 'I expected you earlier,' he said, as he led Jared and Fred Steele to his private office. 'Well, nowadays people just don't seem to believe punctuality is important any more.'

That was all. Jared could have taken it up, as undoubtedly George Alexander would have, but he knew Morgan better. In fact, the old banker was actually in rather good spirits this morning. He proved it by offering to have his girl bring in coffee if either of his visitors wished for any.

Neither did.

Jared got down to facts and figures without any waste of time. There was one interruption: Miss Jorgenson called him in Morgan's office to say Sergeant Hopper had telephoned a few moments earlier to leave a rather enigmatic message.

'He said, sir, that the ball had been satisfactorily intercepted. He also said that would make sense to you. Does it, Mr. Dexter?'

Jared smiled at Miss Jorgenson's tone of gentle bewilderment. 'It makes sense,' he told her, and rang off. *Carling was alive!* Hopper had intercepted his reply to the pseudo Niarchos-cablegram. Jared's spirits began climbing. He was almost jovial before he'd finished acting as intermediary between Steele and Morgan.

But his surmise back at the office had been very close to accurate. By the time he left the bank, found a decent restaurant in the financial district and got a table, it was past one o'clock.

The luncheon was pleasant, light, and

nourishing. He broke a personal rule and topped it off with a pint of beer, as a sort of celebration about the Carling affair.

Later, riding comfortably through city traffic in a taxi, he went over his scheme to entice Carling home, and it seemed plausible unless of course Carling and Niarchos got into cable or telephonic communication, and then he'd be in serious trouble.

For the first time, he had a chilly moment to reflect upon the consequences of what he was doing, with nothing to interrupt these rather grisly thoughts. Shortly before the taxi delivered him to the door of the Niarchos building, he decided to suggest to Sergeant Hopper that perhaps a very discreet armed bodyguard might not be out of order, and further, that Sergeant Hopper make damned sure Carling and Niarchos didn't contact one another.

The Niarchos Building was a very modern steel-glass-and-aluminium structure that shone with cleanliness, which was unusual enough in itself, but it also had entire walls of windows, and its interior was just as modern even to the lifts, which were swift enough at putting Jared on the tenth floor to leave his stomach slightly queasy.

Niarchos's private offices were heavily carpeted. The reception office was so silent it had to be sound-proofed, and the darkly alluring woman who smiled at Jared, seemed perfectly matched to the mahagony, teak, and dark walnut that gave everything an atmosphere of richness, of almost Oriental splendour, and that complete quiet.

The handsome woman took Jared through two rooms where people worked at desks, and lightly knocked upon a carved door beyond. It opened without a sound. Jared saw Niarchos take his hand from beneath the edge of his desk as he rose, smiling. The alluring secretary walked off without another look, or a sound.

'Right on time,' beamed Niarchos, stepping around his huge, carved desk to push a leather chair up close for Jared. 'I like that, Jared.' He motioned towards the chair, 'Please...'

Back again behind the desk, Paul Niarchos eased down, picked up a folder from a pile of other folders and lay it within Jared's reach. 'What I need right now,' he said, speaking briskly and frankly, as though they already had an established relationship, 'is for you to take over this end of my affairs, Jared. Inside this folder are the financial fruits of a number of personal deals I've made over the past few years. They are separate from my other business affiliations, you see, so there'd be no point in my turning them over to my organizational book-keepers.'

Jared wondered about those private deals enough not to point out that if Niarchos needed an accountant, perhaps for tax purposes, Jared was not his man. As an attorney he knew the tax laws, but his speciality was quite different.

He did not say any of this, though, and Niarchos went on saying what he wanted, until, having made himself clear, he looked up enquiringly. 'All right?'

Jared nodded. 'All right. But I'll have a professional accountant put these matters into order before I review them from the tax levels.'

Paul Niarchos smiled amiably, his dark gaze as inscrutable as always. 'Very good.' He rose. 'Jared, have you ever tried Turkish coffee?'

Jared never had although he'd heard people who knew say it was similar to the chicory-coffee of New Orleans, and he'd had just enough of that to dislike it. He rose and mentioned some fictitious appointment he had later in the afternoon.

Niarchos laughed, returned to his desk and said, 'If a person doesn't like Turkish coffee, they can't stand it. All right. Now I know this much about your personal tastes.' His smile dwindled but the black eyes continued to study Jared. 'Suppose, from time to time, I wanted you to take little trips for me ...' He sat waiting Jared's answer, and when it seemed a bit slow coming, he added more to what he'd already said.

'They would have to do with these little separate deals I make from time to time, Jared. You see, I've been a money-chaser all my life, and it's hard to break lifelong habits. In other words, when I'm abroad I occasionally see opportunities that are outside my usual scope. That's when I get involved in these other things, you see, but now they've grown until—well—when you've read through that folder you'll see what I mean—they've grown until I can no longer simply play with them like a hobby.'

Jared was considering his answer very carefully. He hadn't deposited the cheque for a quarter of a million dollars yet. It was still locked in the top drawer of his desk. He was positive that before very much longer Paul Niarchos was going to be in very serious trouble over one, and perhaps two, murders. Niarchos would sooner or later discover what Jared's part had been in all this. As Jared saw his present position, he had to play a part without getting too deeply involved.

He finally said, 'Paul, as you know, I have my other clients. It just isn't possible for me to drop everything I've worked at building up for ten years and more, to spend a good deal of time on your affairs. If you really need a full-time attorney I'd like to suggest—'

'Jared, it won't take that much of your time, believe me.' Niarchos rose as though to emphasize what he was saying. 'Primarily, I need someone who has access to the best social circles. You have that. I also need someone whose views are similar to mine, and finally, I want a man I can trust.'

Jared forced a little smile. 'That's very flattering. If these little trips don't push me too hard, of course I'll undertake them for you.'

Niarchos's smile bloomed and his jet-black eyes shone with returned brightness. 'Good. Now, you're in a hurry, and as a matter of fact so am I. So suppose you take the folder along, study it, and when I need you again, you'll be able to give me some constructive advice, eh?'

Afterwards, going down again in one of those bullet-like lifts, Jared tried to figure out where the truth had parted from the affectation, up there, but try as he might he could not make the differentiation.

He returned to his office in a taxi, was informed by Miss Jorgenson that there had been no calls since the one from Hopper, and took Paul Niarchos's private file-folder into his office to study.

He didn't know what to expect, but he had the feeling of a treasure-hunter who had just stumbled on to a secret cave that promised to hold all manner of breath-taking revelations.

He even neglected to telephone Sergeant Hopper although that had been one of his intentions the moment he got back to the office.

CHAPTER EIGHTEEN

THE NEARING CLIMAX

The Niarchos file was interesting, in fact Jared would have said it was intriguing because it showed how a man whose obsessive motivation had always been the acquisition of wealth, couldn't even pass up opportunities that to other men of great wealth would have seemed time-wasting and trivial.

But it did not mention gold in any way, and it did not so much as imply that Paul Niarchos was involved with that grisly business of procuring—however it was done—dental gold from Nazi murder furnaces.

There wasn't a single case in the Niarchos file that seemed the slightest bit dishonest, nor even unethical, and it was this total lack that finally made Jared toss the file down.

Paul Niarchos was just not that pure. Even when Elizabeth Leeds had been alive, and the international-finance set had clustered round her Hyde Park mansion, Jared had heard enough in quiet comments to know that other very wealthy men knew how Niarchos operated.

In a way, Jared was annoyed that Niarchos would think he had fooled everyone so completely, and that Jared was naïve enough to believe the image projected by the deals in that folder was the real Paul Niarchos.

He had to switch on his desk-lamp before reaching for the telephone to put in a call to Sergeant Hopper. It was getting along towards quitting time.

Hopper wasn't available although his shadow, Detective Harlow was, and in a very pleasant, deep and somehow reassuring voice, he told Jared that Hopper was this very moment on his way across town to see Jared at his office.

There was a wait of something like half an hour, and in the interim Miss Jorgenson left for the day.

It was a good time for reflection, which is what Jared used the interim for. He had a private electric coffee urn in a cabinet, and brewed himself a cup of the liquid, but it didn't taste very good so he unplugged the urn and put the cup aside.

A little later Sergeant Hopper arrived, his usual big, affable, somewhat shambling, and wholly deceptive, self. He had the copy of Carling's cablegram with him.

Jared mentioned monitoring contacts between Niarchos and Carling, only to receive a rather reproving look.

'That was done this morning,' he said. 'You don't have much faith in the Department, do you, Mr. Dexter?'

Jared had *faith*, he said. It was trust he was a

bit shy of. He then mentioned the bodyguard and again Sergeant Hopper looked down his ample nose.

'You've been covered for several days.'

Hopper then drew a slip of paper from a pocket and offered it. There were three choices of cablegrams worked out in longhand. Jared took the paper to his desk, nearer the lamp, and Hopper took a chair and sighed as though he might be tired, which was a possibility although Jared wasn't greatly concerned.

The cablegrams were all signed 'Niarchos' and in each it was suggested that Carling return to the States. Jared made several minor changes and handed the paper back for Sergeant Hopper's examination. As he did this he said, 'You will be able to pick him up at the airport?'

Hopper raised his eyes. 'Is that wise, Mr. Dexter?'

Jared was too surprised to answer right away. Arresting Carling had been behind everything he'd devised thus far.

Hopper spoke on. 'The best I could manage would be suspicion, Mr. Dexter, and he'd post bail within the hour.'

'Well, you can't leave him loose, Sergeant, for hell's sake, to have him go directly to Niarchos with that cablegram summoning him home in his hand. He's got to be arrested or the whole blasted affair will fall apart.'

Hopper returned to studying the several

drafts to the cablegram as he quietly said, 'Of course I'll have some men at the airport, but you and your friends were so successful before in talking with Mr. Carling ...' Hopper raised his eyes again, and their innocence was so obvious Jared frowned. Hopper folded the paper, pocketed it and resumed speaking in that gentle tone of voice.

'Police interrogation methods, especially since those recent Supreme Court decisions, just wouldn't be very convincing, Mr. Dexter.'

Jared thought a moment then nodded. 'And of course you realize that if George Alexander and I whisk Carling to Hyde Park from the airport, we'll be involved in an abduction.'

'Not necessarily. Not if Carling came willingly, which I'm sure he'd do if he thought for one moment Niarchos hadn't called him home to discuss the Leeds case at all—but rather to harm him because Niarchos now knows Carling informed against him.'

Jared blew out a big breath. Sergeant Hopper was as devious as anyone Jared had ever known. Furthermore, he must have cooked all this up well in advance of coming to Jared's office, which meant Hopper had been a busy lad.

Hopper grinned and a moment later Jared, not quite as pleased, grinned back. 'All right, Sergeant. We'll be there to tell Carling for his own safety he'd better go to hide in Hyde Park.'

'Very good, Mr. Dexter. Now I'd like to ask one favour: I'd like to be secreted in that house with a police secretary and a listening device to take down anything Carling tells you gentlemen. You know very well that we've got to get some evidence. Some really worthwhile evidence.'

Jared nodded, clasped both hands on the desk and gazed at Sergeant Hopper as he wondered for the dozenth time how he'd ever got himself so deeply involved in all this.

Hopper rose. 'I'll see that the cablegram is sent at once. Then I'll intercept the reply, if there is one, and if there isn't I'll let you know which aircraft he's got to be returning on. That should do it, shouldn't it?'

Jared nodded and rose. The meeting was over. As the two of them left his office Jared flicked off the lamps. On the way down in the lift he said he thought Niarchos either suspected nothing, or else he was a consummate actor.

Hopper had a casual remark to offer about that. 'If Niarchos knew how close he was to disaster, I just can't visualize a man of his cleverness returning the way he's done.'

'Not even for vengeance against the men who wrung that story out of Carling?'

'Not then, especially, Mr. Dexter, because Niarchos could sprinkle a few thousand-dollar bills around this town through any one of his intermediaries, and both you and Mr.

Alexander would end up on refrigerated slabs in the Coroner's cellar within eight hours. No, I don't believe the man suspects a thing—yet.'

As they parted in the darkness outside, Jared could still hear that final word ringing in his head.

He drove to the hotel, had a late dinner, then went to his rooms. Shortly before ten o'clock, when he was thinking about retiring, Sergeant Hopper buzzed him.

'An unexpected stroke of good luck, Mr. Dexter: Carling answered the cablegram within an hour of receiving it. He'll be arriving at the airport on the mid-day flight from London.'

Jared rang off, showered, and sat on the edge of his bed for fifteen minutes before dialling Fred Steele, who came to the telephone grumpily, and told Fred to meet him at nine in the morning at the Leeds mansion. He didn't explain. His next call was to George, who wasn't in bed yet. Very briefly, Jared explained what was happening, promising to give full details in the morning. George was perfectly agreeable. He actually sounded pleased, and promised to have a big breakfast ready when Fred and Jared arrived.

That offer made Jared grimace as he eased back into bed. The least fascinating thing he could think of right at the moment was food.

Sleep came belatedly but it came. However, it did not linger past six in the morning, so

Jared had plenty of time to dress carefully and also to review what lay ahead.

He told himself, as he descended to the garage and got his car, that he had to be upon the verge of lunacy to be planning an abduction. And regardless of what Sergeant Hopper had said it *was* kidnapping. The law had a somewhat less elastic definition than Sergeant Hopper had. It said somewhat specifically that if a person, minor or not, were enticed away through the use of force, violence, *or deception*, the crime was abduction.

'Of *all* people,' he told the empty car as he hastened towards the Leeds mansion, 'an attorney!'

George was up and rather cheerful. He reported that his father, after a particularly bad time the day before, had spent a good night. He also said he now had a full-time physician with his father, as well as the full-time nurse.

They went to the study to await Fred. There, Jared explained what they were going to attempt. When he said Sergeant Hopper was favourable, George's dark brows shot upwards.

'I had him pegged as quite different. In fact, I'd about come to the conclusion he was our biggest stumbling block, Jared.'

There was a frank answer for that. Jared used it. 'Right this minute I wish he were.'

Fred arrived and the three of them went to breakfast. Jared went through it all again for Fred's benefit, and at once Steele had a comment to make.

'This thing seems to be coming down to the wire, so excuse me if I make a personal point. Suppose we all land in trouble with the law? Suppose Carling doesn't come through? Sergeant Hopper—who is perfectly in the clear—denies any knowledge of what we're going to do—and the sky falls on us. Look, I work for a living. Not as a society lawyer and not as heir to eighty million dollars.'

George grinned. It seemed to Jared that the only time he *really* did that, was when there was some sort of crisis at hand. 'I've got what may be part of a solution, Fred. Once I offered you a quarter of a million dollars, remember?'

Steele's ironic look came up. 'No one is ever likely to forget something like that—ever.'

'You're going to get it as soon as this thing is all cleared up. Wages, if you like.'

Fred ate for a moment then showed his companions a little lopsided smile. 'I'm ready, gentlemen, any time you two are.'

Jared didn't comment on George's magnanimity. He thought it excessive, but he was also privately pleased. As for his own position, he shrugged it off. As an attorney he had been trained to do one thing people untrained in the law seldom did—he was trained to not even start worrying until the sky actually *did* fall.

After breakfast Jared led them back to the study. There, he checked in with Miss Jorgenson. When she said no one had telephoned thus far, he left word for her to ask Sergeant Hopper to get in touch with him at the Leeds mansion.

It was a tedious and nerve-tingling long wait, but just as George was beginning to denounce Hopper, the sergeant called in. Carling's flight-number was given to Jared, plus the time of arrival at Kennedy Airport. Hopper did not offer any encouragement; he neglected even to wish Jared good luck. All he said was: 'Ask Mr. Alexander to instruct his servants what to do when two policemen show up in an hour or so. Also, ask him to give his people the rest of the day off, if that's agreeable with him.'

Jared passed on the instructions and George left the study to implement them. When he returned it was time to leave for the airport. George had an ominous bulge beneath his coat and Jared pointed to it.

'Leave it,' he ordered.

George lifted the coat to disclose a stubby-barrelled pistol. He protested against Jared's order but even Fred was shaking his head now.

'Leave it!' Jared said, snarling the words this time. 'George, this isn't California. In New York City you're not even supposed to own one of those things. And if there's trouble at the airport we most certainly don't want to compound it with a violation of the Sullivan Gun Law. Now put that damned thing in a desk drawer and *leave it here!*'

Alexander sulkily complied, but as soon as they marched out of the house his spirits rose again. Obviously, George was one of those rare people who reacted to peril with bursts of energetic exuberance.

Jared wasn't. As he climbed beneath the wheel of his car, the others getting in the back, he told himself for the last time today that he simply had to be partially unsound to be embarking upon what they were starting out to do!

CHAPTER NINETEEN

WELCOME HOME!

The airport was large and perhaps the most hectic time to be there searching for someone was mid-day when most of the aircraft from Europe were due to arrive.

On the other hand that was also an ideal time of day providing someone had in mind becoming lost in crowds.

Jared had allowed a little more time than it had turned out was required. He'd anticipated more traffic-trouble, perhaps a delay in Carling's flight, and of course the snarl of people at the airport. But perversely, the traffic, although heavy, was not troublesome and as they parked the car and walked on into the reception-building, the flight upon which Carling was arriving, was announced as being on-time. Finally, Jared knew which point of debarkation would be Carling's because he had used it many times himself.

They actually had a while to wait and as Fred Steele lit a cigarette he lowered his head slightly and said, 'Unless I'm very much mistaken, that's a cop over across the corridor reading the newspaper. And if you'll look around I think you'll see other idlers who seem to pretty well fit police specifications.'

Jared knew because Hopper had told him, there would be policemen about. He brushed that aside as though it were unimportant and concentrated on watching the clock. Carling's flight would arrive in less than fifteen minutes.

Fred was less impervious to the idea of police surveillance, and even after Jared explained that those men were on hand solely to ascertain that Carling actually arrived, Fred still seemed uneasy.

People by the hundreds walked past, some heading for the flight ramps, some for the distant taxi-stands, luggage in hand, while others seemed to be friends or relatives hastening in search of someone who would be arriving.

There was a rather numerous coterie of these

greeters, as was always the case, particularly where overseas flights were involved, and as luck willed it, with something like ten minutes to wait at the debarkation area where Elbert Carling would appear, a large, vociferous and straggling family of them arrived to swell the otherwise quiet and patient crowd.

To Jared their alien language made no sense whatever, but their short, dumpy, shapeless figures plus their liquid dark eyes and features in general put him in mind of Syrians, Lebanese, Armenians, something like that. George Alexander viewed them with impassive interest and Fred, exhaling bluish smoke, seemed more annoyed than anything else by their arrival.

They talked loudly and endlessly in that outlandish tongue, and a burly man, very swarthy and perhaps half a head taller than the others who seemed to exert some kind of control, or leadership, turned with a friendly and apologetic smile and said, 'After twenty years a cousin comes.' He made a gesture with his hands that was pure Middle East in its imploring appeal. Fred smiled without much genuine warmth and nodded as though he understood. Jared looked at George. They grinned slightly.

An overhead loud-speaker announced the approach of Carling's flight. It also gave the place of origin, scheduled arrival—which coincided perfectly—and told which ramp the debarking passengers would use as they entered the terminal.

Fred Steele dropped his cigarette, stepped upon it, shifted position slightly to permit the crowding-up Armenians or whatever they were to get between him and the ramp, then turned slightly and gazed over the heads of those babbling aliens. Jared and George were lounging nearer a large smooth stone pillar. They, too, let people filter on past, getting closer to the ramp.

An amber light glowed above the landing-ramp, but although the Armenians trilled happily, no one came through. The man who had spoken to Fred earlier turned with a questioning look. Fred leaned down and said, 'Customs. It'll be a little while yet.'

He was right, of course, although the information that spokesman for the Armenians interpreted for them did not seem to satisfy their garrulous complaints very much.

Then a handsome woman appeared at the upper end of the ramp wearing a mink coat although it was June and quite warm out. She gazed with candid distaste at the crowd of people waiting at the other end of the ramp. When a grey and distinguished man joined her, bags in hand, she started forward. Those two were the first debarkees. Others came, singly and in pairs, looking rumpled and in some cases, tired. Finally a burly, swarthy man started down the ramp carrying two canvas bags, an overcoat, and the remains of a net pouch containing fruit, and those Armenians came to life again, noisily calling and waving. The rumpled man's lined face broke into a wide smile, more it seemed of relief than of welcome.

Directly behind him came Elbert Carling.

Jared moved slightly, so that the stone pillar partially concealed him. Across the way Fred Steele dropped his head slightly and mingled with the exuberant Armenians. George Alexander stepped to one side of the ramp and became engrossed with a time-table hanging in a picture-frame upon the wall.

Carling was carrying a light coat over one arm while in the other hand he had an overnighter. If that was all his luggage he was travelling light. Near the end of the ramp he paused to cast a searching glance all around, then, evidently satisfied, he resumed his march towards the area where crowding people, including the vociferous Armenians, filled an area of perhaps a hundred feet. When he stepped to the marble floor and turned, heading in the direction of a street exit, Jared, George and Fred fell in behind him.

Jared knew those plainclothes policemen would be observing all this. It was even possible they'd be carrying concealed transmitters which would enable them to keep in touch with Sergeant Hopper.

The sun was bright, outside the airport

terminal where waiting taxis were lined up at the kerb, their drivers lounging indolently, confident of fares. Also, there was a diminishing crowd outside, so Jared moved in when Carling put down his overnighter, switched the light raincoat to his other arm and raised a wrist to glance at his watch.

'You have lots of time,' he said, 'and we have a car waiting.'

Carling gave a little start when he recognized Jared. He also saw Fred Steele and as though that indicated there might be another one, he turned from the waist and met George Alexander's gunmetal gaze.

Carling dropped his arm. 'What are you doing here?' he demanded.

George smiled faintly. 'Welcoming committee. Like Jared said, we have a car waiting.'

Carling's surprise had passed. He looked elsewhere, as though anticipating additional greeters. There were none. Jared stooped, picked up the overnighter and jerked his head. 'Follow Fred, Mr. Carling. Don't make a scene and we'll be just another big happy family.'

'I'm not going with you,' snapped Carling, and Fred Steele stepped closer, his face up close.

'You're going with us, Mr. Carling, and there is no one else here to meet you. Does that ring any little bells in your head?'

Carling recoiled from Fred's closeness,

colliding with George who had moved up behind him. 'Carling, Niarchos doesn't know you're here. He thinks you're still in Europe.'

Finally, the look of comprehension showed in Carling's ashen face. He sought Jared and said, ' *You* did it.'

Instead of answering Jared jerked his head again and reached to propel Carling along with a little push. The four of them walked easterly along the sidewalk towards the huge, paved parking area. Nothing more was said.

People were leaving the airport in droves, some laughing, some as noisy as those Armenians, who evidently had arrived in four or five cars because now they were engaged in an arm-waving dispute about which vehicle their cousin should ride in.

When Carling was too far from the terminal to cry out, he stopped and looked hard at Jared. 'Getting me back here like this can make you an accessory if anything happens to me.'

Jared wasn't impressed. 'Why the hell did you run out on us in the first place—if not to warn Niarchos, whom you evidently knew was in Paris?'

'I didn't tell Paul Niarchos a thing. Not a single thing.'

'But you saw him in Paris, Elbert.'

'I saw him, yes. After all, we move in the same—'

'Get along,' growled George. 'We'll talk at home.'

Carling turned. 'You'd better know what you're doing, Mr. Alexander. Kidnapping is a very serious offence in this—'

'Look behind you,' said Jared. 'Do you see those men back there watching us?' It was those plainclothes detectives who had been waiting at the embarkation ramp. 'In case you didn't see them before, Carling, they were also waiting when you came off the aeroplane. If you want, we'll get in our car and drive back without you. But you'd better recognize the fact that you're too far from the terminal to get help.'

Carling squinted back where several lounging men stood among the parked cars. 'Who are they?' he breathed.

Fred, taking over from Jared, said, 'I'll bet you a thousand to one every one of them is armed.'

Carling kept studying the distant, unmoving strangers. 'No,' he whispered. 'Why would he do that? I didn't tell him anything.'

George grunted dourly. 'You didn't have to, Carling. You weren't the only one who could have told him. Remember what you told us that night before you skipped out? Now there were four of us who knew.'

Carling's eyes whipped to George. 'You didn't,' he said, and George shrugged.

Jared tapped Carling's arm. 'Take your pick. Them or us. With us you'll get a ride to Hyde Park. With them ...' Jared became

178

interested in watching the Armenians finally resolve their dispute and begin to clamber noisily into several cars.

Carling made his decision. 'Let's go. Which is your car?'

As Jared slid under the wheel, with Fred riding in front beside him, he grimaced. So, technically, it hadn't been abduction; Carling had asked them to take him along. But there was that provision in the law about deception. They had certainly used deception to the hilt, intimating that those plainclothes detectives back there were killers hired by Niarchos.

Traffic did not favour them on the drive back as it had on the drive out, but it could have been worse; at least the ant-like processions of commuters weren't around.

There was June heat, too, along with an unusual sun-glare. Usually, that pall of smog that hung just above the city obscured direct sunrays. Today, probably because there had been upper-atmosphere turmoil during the night, the pall was little more than a diaphanous veil which would eventually thicken, but which at the time they drove towards Hyde Park did little or nothing about filtering the sunshine.

Carling rode in the back with George Alexander, and throughout the entire drive he only spoke once, that was when he asked Fred Steele for a cigarette.

Otherwise, he seemed to draw constantly
179

deeper inside himself. George's attempts at engaging him in conversation failed, and Jared, occupied with the driving, was content to have it that way. If Carling began talking now, he'd simply have to repeat it again at the Leeds mansion where Sergeant Hopper was by now concealed with his police secretary and his recording device.

They reached the mansion, finally, with the heat making itself felt more than ever. As Carling alighted he fished for a handkerchief and dabbed at his face with it. There was a possibility that his perspiration was not altogether a result of the heat.

Fred brought along the overnighter as the four of them left the car, and George, preceding the little entourage, opened the door and led the way towards the distant study.

Carling finished his cigarette as he halted near a chair and bent to crush it in an ashtray. Fred, the last one, gently closed the study door, put the overnighter to one side and remained in front of the door as though to make certain no one would leave the room.

It may have been a useless gesture because Carling simply dropped into a chair and studied the others, seemingly with no will left for escaping, but it also left no one in doubt that this was anything but a friendly little social gathering.

George strolled to the window, gazed out briefly, then turned and stood, hands in pockets, gazing with what could have been an air of detached interest at Elbert Carling.

CHAPTER TWENTY

A PROMISE OF AMNESTY

Carling said, 'Listen to me; I've told you all I can tell. And the reason I fled was because of exactly what I was afraid you'd do—and evidently you've done it—got word to Paul Niarchos about what I said. I'm grateful for small mercies; you told him *after* he returned from Paris.'

'You'd have warned him if you'd had the guts,' said George, from over by the window. 'What happened when you met him in Paris?'

'Nothing happened,' shot back Carling. 'We met, had dinner together, and talked. That was all.'

'Lost your courage,' said George.

Carling didn't deny it. 'All right, have it your way. I lost my courage. As I tried to explain the last time we four talked in this house, I had a lot to lose.'

'Like your life,' growled George, and smiled coldly. 'But you didn't tell it like it was, Carling.'

'What are you talking about, Alexander?'

'You killed Elizabeth Leeds!'

181

Carling sat like stone, twisted in his chair as he stared at George Alexander. Finally, no longer speechless, he faced Jared. 'What tommy rot. Do you believe that, Jared?'

There was no immediate response as Carling and Dexter sat looking squarely at one another, but eventually Jared inclined his head. 'There is enough proof,' he said. 'And there is something else as well—the fact that Niarchos will say you killed her if he's got into a corner, Elbert.'

'Why?' demanded Carling, throwing up both arms in desperate enquiry. 'Why would I kill her? I—was extremely fond of Elizabeth.'

'So was Niarchos,' put in Fred, from over at the door.

'You're drunk,' exclaimed Carling in a voice that was getting both loud and shrill. 'You've been imagining things. Why would I kill her? And there is something else—Paul Niarchos strangled those men in Europe; this is definitely his way of—'

'We know all that,' said Jared a trifle sharply. 'We know how he killed those people in Europe. We know what it was he held over your head to make you kill Elizabeth—that investigation you clumsily undertook for Mrs. Leeds, using the name of Jones. We know Niarchos offered you a choice—he'd kill you unless you agreed to kill her.'

Carling dug out the white handkerchief and dabbed at his blanched face. He did not react with outrage at these accusations. In fact he only reacted to what Jared was saying by dabbing at his face in a wordless sweat.

'And we also know what happened to David Leeds. His body has been exhumed and examined. Do you want to hear more, Elbert?'

Carling turned towards Fred Steele. 'Another cigarette?' Steele went forward to give Carling the cigarette and afterwards to flick the lighter for him. He did this without speaking and then returned to his post by the door as though Carling hadn't spoken at all.

George Alexander left his place by the window, strolled over, still with both hands in his trouser pockets, and stood studying Carling. In the circumstances George's stance, his stone-steady staring, could not have done much for Carling's peace of mind. Finally, George said, 'Too bad New York doesn't have a death-row, Carling. Too bad.'

Carling shot Alexander an apprehensive look, then quickly swung his attention to Jared. 'What do the police know?' he asked.

Jared shrugged. As far as he was concerned none of what had thus far been said gave Sergeant Hopper, listening in, enough from *Carling*, to make a good arrest. Jared said, 'What difference does that make?'

'A lot,' shot back Carling, his body stiffening slightly as he leaned forward. 'Listen to me for a moment: I'll put one million dollars cash in a packet and hand it you for dividing up, if you'll take me to my bank, then drive me back to the airport.' He hung there looking at Jared, and when he got no response in that area, he swung towards Fred, and finally towards George Alexander. 'You hardly knew her,' he said to Alexander. 'You owe her nothing anyway. What did she do for you, but keep you out of sight so you wouldn't cramp her style and make her seem to be something she never wanted to be—a mundane mother?'

George nodded. 'Granting all that is true, what do you suppose I need with an additional third of a million dollars? Carling, I've already got eighty million.'

That left Carling with nothing to say; it was the truth. George Alexander, by inheritance one of the richest men in America, did not need more money. Carling raised his face to Jared again, imploringly this time.

'All right. If the money isn't enough, I'll offer you something else: the truth about David Leeds.'

'The truth about you and *Elizabeth* Leeds,' said Jared.

Carling, interpreting this to mean Jared might accede, said, 'But you've got to give me your word you'll deliver me to the airport.'

Fred made a cruel snort of a laugh and George, turning in obvious disgust, strode to a chair and dropped down. Only Jared didn't react with scorn. He said, 'You tell us *everything*, Elbert, starting at the beginning.'

Carling's glimmer of hope strengthened. Concentrating exclusively on Jared he said, 'Your word?'

Jared nodded. 'My word. We'll deliver you back at the airport.'

Carling leaned back and looked at the other two. George was as impassive as he occasionally became while Fred, frowning, kept his eyes on Jared. Fred was perplexed, but he said nothing.

Carling relaxed a little. 'Will *they* go along?' he asked, nodding towards Fred and George.

Jared nodded. 'They will go along. Now get on with it.'

Carling licked his lips. He seemed most desperately to want to trust Jared, but he also seemed afraid to. Then he spoke again. 'I'm putting my trust in your word, Jared. All right. Go back to the year before David Leeds died—and you are right, he didn't die of a heart attack, but that's part of the story. He and Paul Niarchos funded that illicit traffic in dental gold from the German death furnaces. I say illicit because while dealing in raw gold was not illegal then, it *was* against the law to smuggle gold out of Germany at that time. Still, it was done. Paul and David put up the money. They knew if they didn't someone else would. The smuggling was so successful however, that within a year they had made a profit in excess of six million dollars. That's when they quarrelled. David didn't want to re-invest in

Europe. He wanted his share converted to negotiable securities so he could bring them to the States. Paul, already with more European and Middle East contacts than American contacts, would not agree. In fact, Paul finally refused even to give David his share. It was at this moment that David died. Not of the heart attack Paul paid one million dollars to have the physician certify on the Death Certificate. David was strangled to death.'

Jared nodded. This far Elbert Carling had told the truth. 'Go on,' he said.

'I think David must have mentioned to Elizabeth that Paul was being troublesome. She may have suspected how he'd died although as far as I know she never mentioned it. But last year she hired me exactly as I've already told you, to look into that gold business.'

'And Paul Niarchos learned about you from some of the men in Europe you paid to talk.'

'Yes.'

'And...'

'Well, he met me at my hotel in New York a month after I'd returned to the States.' Carling paused to shoot a worried look at George. 'I don't like to tell the rest.'

George sneered. 'Why not? You said yourself I had no reason to love her. Go on.'

'Paul told me what he knew, and of course I already had heard about Paul's killings in Europe. I was deathly afraid.' Carling mopped his face again and Fred Steele, unasked, provided him with another cigarette. Then he went on. 'He would take a trip to Mexico City for a week and when he returned if I hadn't killed Elizabeth he would have me killed—slowly, he said, and very painfully.'

'You killed her?'

Carling nodded, and now he kept his face averted from George. 'I was at the party the night she died. I made certain the glass door leading from the conservatory to the garden was unlocked. I even went outside to look round the garden, but the gardener was over by a bulb bed smoking his pipe and looking around, so I slipped back inside. Later, after everyone had left, I returned ... I got upstairs without any difficulty. Elizabeth—was brushing her hair. I slipped over beside her and ... and knocked her out of the chair ... then, using her own hair I killed her.'

'By strangulation,' said Jared. 'So if anything was ever to come up, it would look like Paul's way of handling dangerous enemies.'

'Well, isn't it enough to say that I killed her?'

'A question,' said George in a flat tone of voice. 'Why were you so afraid of Niarchos, since *you* killed Mrs. Leeds, not him?'

Carling wiped his face with the handkerchief as he replied. 'You don't know Niarchos very well, obviously. I did intend to warn him, when we met in Paris, but seeing him there when I had no idea he wasn't still in New York was a terrible experience. For a moment I was terrified; he could have been pursuing me. Then he said he'd been in Paris a week and seemed genuinely glad to see me. I was so relieved ... It was like being given back my life ... I didn't mention what I'd done.'

Jared looked from Fred to George, and rose from his seat behind the desk. 'On your feet,' he said to Carling, and when the murderer limply obeyed and stood there looking with a grey face and dry eyes from one man to the other other, Jared said, 'You want to come along, George, while we deliver him to the airport?'

Alexander rose nodding his head. 'I'll come. But first I've got to go upstairs and check on my father.'

The moment George was out of the room Carling said, 'He'll call the police, Jared! My gawd you've got to stop him!'

The man's nerves were perilously near the shattering point. Instead of replying to Carling, Jared said, 'Fred, Mr. Carling needs a double shot of straight bourbon. We'll wait for it by the front door.' Then, as Steele also left the room, Jared motioned for Carling to start walking.

The killer was indeed in a state bordering on collapse. It wasn't altogether attributable to what had transpired in the study either; he'd been living with a nightmare for a long time.

When he turned frantically, to implore Jared

188

again, Dexter shook his head and gave Carling a slight shove. 'No one is going to call the police. I gave you my word and I'll keep it. You'll be delivered to the airport.'

Fred returned with a brimful glass which Carling took with greed and downed in two big swallows. Any other time it might be logically assumed that much straight bourbon would have made him stagger or gasp. This time even his colouring did not improve until, over by the front door, George came to join them.

They went to the car through mid-day sunsmash. The heat did what a badly depressed nervous system had utterly failed to do for Carling. He had a little trouble untracking his feet when he climbed into the back of the car and dropped limply against the cushions.

This time, George rode in front with Jared and Fred Steele rode at the back. This time too, the traffic was mostly laden lorries, taxis, and a few private vehicles, but not enough of them in all categories to impede Jared's steady course back towards the airport.

Once, Jared and George looked at one another, but no signal passed from one to the other; they just quietly gazed at one another, and afterwards Jared concentrated on his driving.

They had to stop for Fred to buy two packets of cigarettes, one for himself, one for Carling, but that was the only interruption in their steady but not very fast drive to the airport. In fact, when they finally arrived there, it was almost one-thirty in the afternoon.

Jared drove directly to the front entrance of the modernistic terminal, stopped and waited while Fred got out along with Elbert Carling, and handed the overnighter to the murderer. None of them spoke, but at the very last moment Carling leaned down and looked imploringly at Jared. 'No double-cross,' he said, making a whine of it. Fred was back in the car so Jared simply engaged gears and drove away without even looking up.

CHAPTER TWENTY-ONE

THE BREATH OF DEATH

The anxiety was a bit much for Fred Steele. Leaning across the back of the front seat as Jared drove down through the parking area, he said, 'Well ...?'

Jared didn't answer until he'd found a slot, had parked with the car facing the terminal's front entrance. Then all he said was, 'Everything mesh, George?'

Alexander nodded. 'Like clockwork. Sergeant Hopper was notifying someone on a two-way intercom when I entered the room. His secretary was already packing up the tape recorder. Any minute now they ought to get

Carling.'

Fred blew out a big, ragged sigh and threw himself back against the cushions without speaking. Like his companions, Steele was now concentrating on the terminal's glass-enclosed front wall where those heavy doors were.

Jared had parked in the first available slot but even so there was a fair bit of distance between the terminal's entrance and the car. Also, people, droves of them, kept hastening into the building from all directions, and also departing from it.

Fred said it would help if they walked up a little closer. Neither of the men in the front seat responded to that so Fred leaned across the back of the front seat to repeat it, and Jared said, 'Be a hell of a note if Hopper blew it.'

Alexander scoffed. 'How? He had plenty of time to have his men here. Moreover, if they delayed, Hopper's still going to have plenty of time; you can't just trot in there and climb right aboard a plane bound for Europe.'

Fred pointed. 'Are those cops?'

Two burly men had just climbed out of a dark car at the terminal's front entrance. While one of them bent down to speak to the driver, his companion stood erect, looking around. He was wearing a checked sports coat, was hatless, and had his eyes adequately concealed behind a pair of over-sized dark glasses.

Jared was sure those two weren't policemen. He even went so far as to dismiss them with a

191

curt comment. 'Ten dozen like those two pass through here everyday. They're a little out of the ordinary, but...'

George and Fred looked over. George said, 'But ...?'

Jared reached for the door-handle. 'Let's go,' he growled, and the three of them left the car briskly, heading back for the air terminal.

Of course it was entirely possible that when they reached the waiting area for overseas passengers, they weren't going to find Elbert Carling because the police had taken him into custody. And there was no reason, or so Jared told the others as they hiked along, to be worried simply because they hadn't seen detectives hustling Carling out of the terminal; there was more than one door to the place.

Inside, they nearly collided with Sergeant Hopper himself. He was standing inconspicuously over near a luggage counter. They didn't question his being here. He'd had ample time. Nor did they question how he'd got past their vigil, because at the distance they'd been keeping it, *individual* people hadn't been close enough to be recognized at all; what they'd been watching for had been a coterie of, perhaps two men flanking a third man.

Hopper smiled but he looked slightly pained too, when the three of them came over to where he was standing. He didn't wait for the questions but nodded gently in the direction of the glassed-in restaurant.

Elbert Carling was sitting there nervously twisting a cup round and round. Now and again he'd raise his eyes to the glass partition and swiftly, searchingly, look at all the nearby people.

Jared turned on Hopper. 'What in the hell are you waiting for?'

Hopper continued to stand placidly watching Carling. 'I don't know, exactly,' he said. 'Do you see those two men eating cakes with tea on either side of him? Well, they were here when you lads brought him along. They were to report to me the moment Mr. Carling showed up, then grab him.'

'Well?' said Jared.

'Well, they reported as I was hastening down here. But it seems you had a tail when you left Hyde Park. Look a little farther back in the restaurant, back as far as that circular table where two men are having coffee and one of them, facing us, is reading a newspaper. Well, my men reported those two arrived five minutes behind you and discreetly attached themselves to Carling.' Hopper looked briefly and reproachfully at Jared. 'Now you know why we haven't arrested Carling.'

'I don't,' said George. 'If those two really are watching him, what are they watching him for, and what difference does it make anyway?'

Hopper smiled indulgently. 'That's exactly what I want to find out.'

Jared, looking at those five men in the

restaurant, could only surmise that somehow, in some way he couldn't fathom quite yet, Niarchos had found out about Carling not only being back in the States, but being in the company of Alexander, Steele, and Dexter.

It didn't dawn on him for a moment that if this were so—if Paul Niarchos had finally got suspicious—then he, himself, was in just as much jeopardy as was Elbert Carling, because Niarchos would also know that he had been in the Leeds mansion with George Alexander, Fred Steele—and Elbert Carling.

He was turning to say something of this when Sergeant Hopper spoke first. 'Carling is leaving. Maybe we'll have some action now. You gentlemen turn away when Carling goes by. I know he'll be distant but let's not blow this now.'

Hopper set the example, becoming much engrossed with a large photograph, in colour, of an immense aeroplane that decorated the rear wall.

Carling strolled towards a large wall-clock to check his wristwatch, then turned and made a slow sweep of the noisy crowd of people on all sides, and finally he walked on. When Jared turned Carling was nearly a hundred feet on along the concourse. Hopper tapped his arm and nodded. Those two strangers were moving in Carling's wake and even as Jared watched, they split up. That was when Sergeant Hopper gave a little grunt of either surprise or disbelief,

194

and looked quickly for his own men. He seemed to suddenly change from his usual large, amiable self, to a different Sergeant Hopper altogether.

The two plainclothesmen were far behind the pair of strangers. Hopper said, 'Too damned far,' and started through the crowd with a rush. Jared jerked his head at George and Fred, then shouldered roughly through in Hopper's wake. He had no idea what had gone wrong but he had faith in Hopper.

The trouble was that by this time the two strangers were on nearly opposite sides of the crowd, and even with the trailing plainclothesmen finally galvanized into action by the example of Sergeant Hopper, they were converging on Hopper and the man he was closing on, not on the other stranger who was moving more rapidly now, on his course to parallel Elbert Carling.

Jared turned when a jostled man snarled. He ignored the offended individual and said, 'George, head for that other one. Try getting behind him. Fred, come with me—we'll try to get in front of him.'

There was no time for explanations but George evidently didn't need one. He veered off while Fred hurried along with Jared.

Hopper finally reached the nearest stranger. It was definitely in his favour that he surprised the man, because as he spoke from a foot behind, the stranger dropped into a crouch and swung round. Hopper didn't wait, he clubbed the man hard, knocking him off-balance. Astonished spectators stopped, gaping, and before the stranger could regain his balance Hopper's two plainclothesmen were there, lunging to grab and hold the man. In all, it had taken something like ten seconds for Hopper's prey to be thoroughly subdued, and afterwards, the man seemed both venomously angry, and surprised.

Jared's prey, because he was moving ahead on an angle, walking rather fast, was less susceptible to apprehension. Still, Jared managed, by hurrying along on a shorter course, to get between the man and Elbert Carling, who was not in such a hurry. There was no sign of George when Jared finally turned and said, 'Head for him, Fred. No, not *that* one; head for Carling. Push him into the crowd.'

Fred obeyed and Jared had one glimpse of Carling's face when Steele grabbed his arm and began pulling him out of the edges of the crowd towards its mainstream. Then Jared saw the second stranger suddenly halt, evidently because he'd seen what Fred had done.

The man was concentrating so hard on Carling he neglected to catch sight of Jared until, less than ten feet distant, Jared saw George emerge from a tangle of people directly behind the stranger. Jared then dropped his shoulder and lunged.

196

The stranger was unprepared for the collision, but even so he reacted as swiftly and violently as his friend had done, and since he hadn't been knocked completely off-balance, he was able to make a more rapid recovery. He cursed, dropped his right hand straight down, and when Jared was ducking down to lunge ahead a second time, George reached, caught the stranger by the collar, whirled him and swung, hard. The blow landed solidly, the stranger's contorted face whipped back, his hat sailed away, and as he fell he dropped something that skidded across the polished floor. It was a revolver with a silencer attached to the barrel.

Jared retrieved the gun and looked up into the startled face of the man at whose feet it had come to rest. Passers-by stopped and gawked.

George flexed his right hand as though the knuckles pained him. He lifted his eyes from the man sprawled unconscious at his feet to Jared, and to the gun Jared was holding up.

'They were going to kill him,' said George, sounding disbelieving. 'I'll be damned.'

A large uniformed policeman was shoving his way through the gathering crowd. Sergeant Hopper was approaching from a different direction. His two plainclothesmen were not in sight. Evidently they had taken the other man away.

Hopper got there one moment after the uniformed officer stopped in front of Jared, looking from the gun to the man lying in front of George Alexander. Sergeant Hopper shoved his I.D. folder up for the uniformed officer to see, said something, and the uniformed man turned without a single word and called upon the crowd to disperse.

Hopper pocketed the silencered weapon, helped George hoist their captive to his feet, and the two of them began struggling towards the front doors with their slack burden.

Outside, with curious people pausing to stare, a police car drew to the kerb. Hopper's plainclothesmen were in it with the manacled prisoner. They climbed out to help load the unconscious man and one of them showed Hopper a second gun with a silencer attached.

'He says they were to receive five thousand dollars each for killing Carling,' explained the plainclothesman. Behind them a man gasped. Jared turned. Carling and Fred Steele were standing there.

Sergeant Hopper stepped back from the car and nodded. It pulled away with its four occupants; then Hopper turned, his face wearing its amiable expression again. 'Close call,' he said, addressing Elbert Carling. 'It was just luck we got them before they got you.'

Carling was badly shaken and fumbled for his packet of cigarettes. This time Hopper held up the lighter, and afterwards he said, 'You know, Mr. Carling, I've been in this business a long time, and it's kind of like baseball. Your enemy has just struck-out once. But he's still entitled to two more strikes.' Hopper pocketed the lighter and turned to Jared, smiling. 'From here on we've got to move fast. Do you suppose your friends would mind taking Mr. Carling to my office downtown while you and I pay Mr. Niarchos a call?'

George answered and Fred nodded agreement. They wouldn't mind at all.

Hopper beamed. 'That's the kind of co-operation the police really appreciate from citizens. Incidentally, one of you ought to ride in the back with him, and it might also be a good idea to frisk him. No point in having him pull a gun at this stage, is there?'

Jared, looking at Fred and George, got a pair of tough smiles. He smiled back as Sergeant Hopper called on him to come along. At this moment Carling finally found his voice.

'He was going to have me killed! Paul was going ...' Carling bit off the words and stared hard at Hopper for a moment, then bleakly nodded his head. 'All right. All right, officer. Now it's my turn. I'll tell you anything you want to know.'

Sergeant Hopper was polite but brief. 'You already have, Mr. Carling. But thanks anyway. Come along, Mr. Dexter, we can't waste much time.'

CHAPTER TWENTY-TWO

THE FINAL APPREHENSION

There wasn't much to say on the drive to the Niarchos Building, but Sergeant Hopper pulled a surprise on Jared when he used his car's transmitter to contact someone down there and ask if Niarchos was still in his office. Whatever reply he got back must have been satisfactory for as Hopper signed off and hung the speaker back upon its dashboard hook, he turned and smiled.

Jared hadn't known Hopper had Niarchos under surveillance. He hadn't thought about it one way or another, but it seemed logical. But Jared *did* mention that unsettling thought he'd had back at the airport.

'Niarchos probably had his own surveillance team. Otherwise, how would he have known Carling had arrived at the Leeds place? And this being so, he also knew I had to be involved because I was out there with Carling.'

Hopper was rather casual about that. 'He had a man watching. We detected him early this morning because we also had watchers on the Leeds mansion. As for your connection with Carling,' Hopper smiled again and whipped round a corner. 'He knew the same way he knew Carling was inside—through his

200

spy. But you weren't in any real danger. I doubted that he'd try to sock you away until he'd first taken care of the one man who could actually testify against him as a confederate. After that, well, we'd have had to come up with something to keep you alive, wouldn't we?'

They parked in a No-Parking zone reserved for loading and unloading lorries in front of the Niarchos Building, and walked briskly into the foyer. Hopper led the way directly to a lift, smiled at the lift-operator and as soon as the doors had closed and the metal box had begun its climb, Hopper said, 'He still hasn't left?'

The lift-operator looked from Hopper to Jared, then shook his head at Sergeant Hopper. 'He's still up there. How did you make out at the airport?'

'Got two men Niarchos sent out to knock off Carling. Got Carling too. I'd say it was a fair morning's work.'

He and the lift-operator smiled, then the box slid to an easy halt and Jared followed Hopper out into the soundproofed corridor. Hopper seemed to hesitate, so Jared said, 'I've been here before. Follow me.'

That alluring dark woman who acted as receptionist smiled at Jared whom she evidently recalled. Her smile froze as Jared leaned across her desk, caught hold of the wire connecting her intercommunication system to the electric wall-plug, and tore the wire loose at the socket.

Afterwards, Jared walked quickly through the other rooms until he came to the electrically-operated private door. He knocked, put his head close and when the faint buzzing sound indicated the door was about to open, he leaned on it.

Paul Niarchos was sitting at his desk looking door-ward. Whatever he'd expected to see when the door silently opened was evidently not what he saw, because he reacted with a quick start.

Behind Jared, Sergeant Hopper spoke softly. 'Sit steady, Mr. Niarchos. Keep both hands on top of the desk and sit steady.'

Niarchos obeyed, although Jared thought surprise made him sit like that, erect and obviously surprised, not Hopper's command.

The sergeant went round behind the desk, hauled Niarchos to his feet, frisked him, then spun him lightly with a powerful hand and shoved him face-forward against the wall. Hopper then went over the desk very carefully without saying a word.

Niarchos said, 'Jared? You'd better not be involved with this fool.'

Hopper looked up. 'Sorry, Mr. Niarchos, I forgot to tell you who I am.'

'I know who you are, Sergeant.'

Hopper smiled. 'That's very flattering, Mr. Niarchos.'

'You won't think so when I finish with you. False arrest will do for a starter. I'll make the city wish it had never heard of you. Brutality too, Sergeant, for the way you hurled me against this wall.'

Jared gave his head a little cynical wag. It sounded like something out of a B movie. He didn't know what he'd expected from Paul Niarchos, the fabulously wealthy international investor, but it wasn't this.

'Turn round,' said Hopper, and motioned for Niarchos to resume his chair behind the desk. 'Just keep the hands on top, if you don't mind.'

Niarchos stared stonily at Jared. 'You got a little out of your league, didn't you?' he asked quietly. 'Jared, you'd better reconsider. I was going to do great things for you; work up to them gradually, but within a couple of years you'd have been a very rich man.' Niarchos's black eyes glittered. 'It's not too late.'

'It's too late,' replied Jared. 'The police have about all they need, Paul.'

Niarchos ignored Hopper and his hard, black stare continued to bore into Jared. 'Carling . . . ?'

Jared nodded. '*And* the pair of goons you sent to kill him.'

Hopper cleared his throat as he went to a chair and sat. 'There is also the man you had watching the Leeds place, Mr. Niarchos, and David Leeds.'

Niarchos reacted with that identical little start of surprise he'd shown when Jared and

203

Hopper had come through the doorway. 'Leeds?' he said. 'What are you talking about, Sergeant?'

'We exhumed him, Mr. Niarchos, some weeks back.' Hopper didn't elaborate. He didn't even pursue that subject. Instead, he said, 'And the German police are very interested in some of your business activities; they're starting an investigation of you in conjunction with the French authorities.' Hopper kept smiling. 'I don't think they'll get the chance, but they've informed us that if through some fluke you escape the murder and complicity charges, they want you for masterminding a gold smuggling ring.'

Niarchos raised a hand from the desktop. When Hopper's smile winked out Niarchos said, 'A cigarette, Sergeant. Only a cigarette.' He fished out the packet, lit up and blew the smoke from a very aromatic Turkish cigarette towards Jared.

'You were in this all along?'

Jared nodded.

Niarchos shrugged. 'Well, I made a mistake with you, didn't I?'

'The ring was closing around you anyway,' said Jared. 'Paul, you didn't have to have Elizabeth killed. You knew her as well as I did. She would never have gone to the police as long as she thought David might be revealed as a dealer in the kind of gold you people were handling.'

204

Niarchos listened, smoked, and kept gazing at Jared for a moment afterwards. Finally he said, 'How did you get Carling back here?'

'That's the nice part about cablegrams, Paul; the signature is printed by a machine.'

Niarchos leaned back. 'Using my name?'

'Yes,' said Jared.

Niarchos let his gaze drift back to Sergeant Hopper. 'You have specific charges?' When Hopper nodded Niarchos made a little shrugging gesture. 'It doesn't matter. I doubt if, in all the history of the world, there have been more than a dozen or so rich men hanged.'

Hopper said, 'If that's all, Mr. Niarchos, why then I guess as far as New York State is concerned, it won't add another victim. For your information New York has outlawed capital punishment. We no longer hang or electrocute people. But if you come out of this with less than ninety-nine years I'll be both very surprised, and very disappointed.'

Niarchos looked faintly amused. 'Ninety-nine years, Sergeant?'

'It's a technicality in the law, Mr. Niarchos. You can't be sentenced to a hundred years imprisonment; the alternative to that is ninety-nine years.'

Niarchos laughed.

Sergeant Hopper chuckled too. 'It *does* sound a little ridiculous doesn't it?' he said. 'But then you see there is another technicality of the law, Mr. Niarchos. Anyone being sentenced for the full ninety-nine years is not eligible for parole.'

Niarchos's smile vanished. Jared, who knew what Hopper had been leading up to, knew also that Hopper was correct. He rose, glanced at his wrist, then said, 'Paul, I'll send back that folder you gave me. Incidentally, I've never cashed your cheque. I'll send that back along with the folder.'

Hopper also stood up. He stepped round the desk and nudged Niarchos. As the shorter, darker man came up out of his chair, Hopper without any ceremony or explanation hauled his arms up behind his back and manacled him like that even though Niarchos roared a curse and made a little outraged struggle to get free.

'It's not at all necessary,' he complained. 'At least permit me to walk through my offices as a gentleman.'

Sergeant Hopper stepped over and picked up the ivory desk-telephone, dialled for an outside line and didn't even turn back to look at his prisoner, let alone answer him.

'Hopper here,' he said briskly. 'Harlow, send along a car to the Niarchos Building armed with riot weapons ... No, there's no trouble, but then we're not out of the building with him yet either. Hurry it up, will you?'

Paul Niarchos grimaced at Hopper. 'What a big coward you are, Sergeant. What do you think—that I have an armoured battalion in

206

the basement, and perhaps snipers at the windows?'

Hopper shrugged and smiled. 'I'll tell you how I've got this close to a pension, Mr. Niarchos. By being careful.'

Jared went to one of the front windows. They were covered by an elaborate bit of ornamental wrought-iron. He wondered whether that was to keep people *out*, or whether it might not be to keep some of Niarchos's visitors *in*.

He didn't ask. He stood looking at the tiny moving figures far below, at the serpentines of crawling traffic, and until then it did not occur to him that most of the day had been spent. He turned back as Paul Niarchos said his name.

'Jared, with you it was all a matter of ethics, eh?'

Jared nodded.

'Well, look at it another way,' said Niarchos. 'I did what absolutely had to be done; this is a world of wolves and the higher you rise in it the more deadly and dangerous they become, so you must be even more deadly or they will rip you to shreds.'

'You don't have to justify anything to me,' exclaimed Jared.

'I think that I do, because you see, I want you on the battery of attorneys who will defend me.'

Jared looked no less surprised than did Sergeant Hopper who was listening to them.

207

Then Jared smiled at Niarchos. 'Sorry, Paul. Not in any circumstances.'

'Not even for that cheque you haven't cashed yet?'

'Not even for that, Paul. Not for five times that much money. What you are, in my book, Paul, isn't worth defending. What in the name of God did you need with more money? You killed people to get more money, for which you had no more need than the man in the moon. I don't think I've ever even heard of a killer like you before, and I know I've never seen one before.'

Hopper went to the window behind Jared, looked down, turned and jabbed towards the door with a stiff thumb. 'Lead the way, Mr. Niarchos.'

For a bit longer Jared and Niarchos stood looking at one another, then the older man turned towards the door, walked over and halted. 'Take the manacles off me,' he said to Hopper, and got a firm shake of the sergeant's head, so then he said, 'Nobody coerces Paul Niarchos. Either you remove the manacles, Sergeant, or I will not take another step.'

Jared thought he knew what was coming. It amused him so he smiled, and Niarchos, seeing that, growled at him. 'Is that so funny, Jared?'

'No, Paul, *that* isn't funny, but the idea of Sergeant Hopper carrying you tucked under his arm through your offices for everyone to see, is *very* funny.'

'He wouldn't,' snapped Niarchos, and turned his head. 'Sergeant, you wouldn't lay a hand upon me.'

Hopper started forward with an unmistakable expression of determination and Niarchos recoiled. 'I'll go,' he said. 'Jared, that overcoat on the rack. Will you fling it around my shoulders?'

To Jared's look of inquiry Sergeant Hopper nodded.

When Paul Niarchos left his office and strolled past the big-eyed people in his outer offices who had doubtless been alerted that something was wrong by the alluring dark receptionist, the hands manacled behind him were hidden very effectively by the coat. He even smiled as he led Jared and Sergeant Hopper out through the offices to the corridor, but as he got into the lift he was unable to keep the smile.

'It can't happen like this,' he muttered in so low a tone that Hopper and the lift-operator, in conversation, did not hear, but Jared heard and lit one of Niarchos's cigarettes for him, stuck it between his lips and looked away.

Downstairs people in the foyer of the building nodded or smiled, or spoke as Niarchos swung past them. As far as Jared could determine, no one was the least bit hostile.

Two plainclothesmen were just outside the large revolving door, and beyond, another pair were standing upon the far side of an unmarked police car.

But nothing happened.

Jared had not thought that anything would happen. He understood Hopper's desire to avoid violence exactly as he appreciated the sergeant's general ability, so when he lent a hand at assisting Niarchos into the rear of the police vehicle, he said, 'No fireworks. What now, Sergeant?'

Hopper straightened up, closed the door on Niarchos, locked it from the outside and motioned for those two men near the revolving door to come forward. 'Take him on in,' he ordered. 'Put a "hold" on him. I'll be along a little later to file the formal charges.' As the men moved away Hopper turned towards Jared, smiling. 'What's next, Mr. Dexter? Well, how about some luncheon, I'm starved.'

Jared grinned in spite of himself.

We hope you have enjoyed this Large Print book. Other Chivers Press or G.K. Hall & Co. Large Print books are available at your library or directly from the publishers.

For more information about current and forthcoming titles, please call or write, without obligation, to:

Chivers Press Limited
Windsor Bridge Road
Bath BA2 3AX
England
Tel. (01225) 335336

OR

G.K. Hall & Co.
P.O. Box 159
Thorndike, Maine 04986
USA
Tel. (800) 223–2336

All our Large Print titles are designed for easy reading, and all our books are made to last.